The Exorcist's Son

OrangeBooks Publication

1st Floor, Rajhans Arcade, Mall Road, Kohka, Bhilai, Chhattisgarh 490020

Website:**www.orangebooks.in**

First Edition, 2024

ISBN: 978-93-6554-872-3

The Exorcist's Son

Alex Jasper Thallapally

OrangeBooks Publication
www.orangebooks.in

"The battle between God and Demons has been a reality since the dawn of human history. Although the Demon knew there is a Living God, it cunningly deceives us from the Maker."

- Alex Jasper

Content

Prologue: The Garden Scene

Jasper woke before dawn, the dim light filtering through the curtains of his room. He lay still, listening to the early morning sounds: the soft chirping of birds outside, the distant hum of traffic. He pushed the covers aside and stepped onto the floor, its cold surface shaking off the last bit of sleep. Another day beginning the same way as the last.

He dressed in a worn half-sleeve shirt and jeans, heading out to the garden behind the house. The garden was his escape, a place where he could focus on the present and not be weighed down by his thoughts.

He took a knife from his workbench and moved to the jackfruit tree. He began chipping the bark, his hands moving in a rhythm that had become second nature to him. The task was familiar, almost automatic, something he did without needing to think.

The sound of gravel crunching behind him made him stop. He turned to see his uncle Isaac approaching, his stride hurried, his face set in a serious expression. Beside him was a man Jasper didn't know. The stranger seemed drained, with tired eyes that suggested he hadn't rested in days.

Isaac approached, a quick nod in Jasper's direction. "Jasper, we need to talk," he said, skipping any greeting. His voice was low and firm, signaling the urgency of whatever news he carried.

Though Jasper now lived in Kochi, his roots randeep here, where family and old bonds still tied him to the place. He wiped his hands on his jeans and nodded toward the man. "Who's this?"

"This is Rudra," Isaac said, gesturing to him. "He's traveled far to see you."

Jasper extended his hand. Rudra shook it, his grip firm but unsteady, his hand cool and damp. The man's nervousness was clear in the tightness of his expression.

"Let's go inside," Jasper suggested, catching a hint of tension in the man's face and realizing this wasn't a casual visit.

Inside, the house was quiet. The walls were covered in photographs, memories from another time that seemed distant now. Jasper's mother, Joyce, was in the kitchen.

She turned as they entered, her smile fading slightly when she saw their faces. Joyce had a way of sensing when things weren't quite right.

"Isaac, Rudra," Jasper introduced. She greeted them, nodding toward the kitchen table. "Have a seat. I'll get you something to drink."

They took seats around the table. Jasper noticed the seriousness in his uncle's expression. Isaac wasn't one to visit without purpose, and Jasper sensed that this wasn't a casual conversation. He waited, composed, his gaze moving between the two men across from him.

Joyce brought cups of tea to the table, her movements slower than usual, careful. Her eyes moved between them, noticing the seriousness in their expressions. Isaac put his cup down gently and the men quietly reached for the warm drinks "We've got a situation in Vagamon," he said, keeping his voice calm but heavy.

The mention of the place brought a flicker of old memories to him, ones he rarely thought about anymore. It had been years since anyone spoke of that place, and he'd preferred to keep it that way. "Rudra and his daughter recently moved from Hyderabad to Vagamon, but their time in the new house has been marked by disturbing events, particularly his daughter's alarming and inexplicable behavior", he continued.

Joyce paused, her hands resting over the table as she listened. Her expression shifted, a quiet seriousness settling in as she looked between them.

"What's going on?" Jasper asked, keeping his voice steady. He hadn't expected anything unusual, but the mention of trouble caught him off guard.

Rudra leaned forward, his face etched with worry. "Please, Jasper. My daughter… she's in trouble. I reached out to Isaac for guidance—he's a pastor, after all—and he said you might be the one who could help."

Jasper felt a knot tighten in his stomach. He barely knew this man and had no idea what kind of trouble his daughter was in. "What do you mean, she's in trouble?" he asked, his voice steady but cautious.

He ran a hand through his hair, the strain evident in his posture. "She's… she's thirteen. Something strange is happening to her, and I don't understand it. I've heard that you might have a way to help her."

Jasper blinked, surprised. "I don't know how I'm supposed to help. I'm not sure I'm the person you're looking for."

Isaac leaned in, choosing his words carefully. "Jasper, I wouldn't ask if I didn't think you could help us get to the bottom of this. That's all I'm asking."

He exhaled, a hint of irritation in his voice. "I'm not sure I'm the right person to handle this, Uncle."

Rudra's desperation seeped into his voice. "I'm begging you. She needs help, and I don't know who else to turn to. I can't lose her."

Jasper looked at his mother, searching her face for guidance. She was silent, but her eyes were filled with a mix of concern and understanding. It was clear she felt the strain of the situation too.

Chapter 1

The Three Men

Fifteen years ago, in the quiet hills of Vagamon, Andrew, Jasper's father, was called to confront a threat that would leave its mark on all involved. Vagamon was a quiet village tucked away in the hills. A few weathered houses dotted the hillside, surrounded by thick forests that lined close to the narrow roads leading in and out. Days in Vagamon blended together, marked only by the steady rhythm of the sun rising and setting.

For most, Vagamon was unremarkable—a place to pass through without much thought. But for Andrew, Jasper's father, it became the final, fateful chapter of his life, a place where duty and darkness met in ways he could never have foreseen. Andrew's work brought him there, leaving an indelible mark on the community.

Andrew was, first and foremost, a pastor. His commitment to his community was steadfast, grounded in a faith that guided him in both simple and challenging times. Over the years, his role slowly evolved.

People sought him out not only for sermons or advice but for help with things they couldn't explain—strange disturbances, hauntings, and troubles that had no clear answers. Andrew began to take on these tasks as a sense of duty, because he felt it was simply part of helping those who came to him.

In his community, Andrew was respected for his courage and dedication, but his work often set him apart. Those close to him knew the toll it took, the burden he carried in silence.

Vagamon tested Andrew in ways he had never expected. It began with a phone call late at night—one of many he had received over the years, but something about this one was different.

The caller's voice was strained, filled with a kind of fear that went beyond the usual. It was the fear of someone who sensed that whatever was happening was far worse than anything they'd encountered before.

As Isaac spoke about these events, his voice was steady, carrying memories that hadn't faded with time. Jasper listened closely, hearing his father's story he had been told before but never truly understood.

Isaac's words brought back feelings Jasper had tried to put behind him, reopening old wounds that hadn't completely healed.

The journey to Vagamon was long and tense. Andrew drove up the narrow, winding road through dense forest, the trees closing in from all sides. When the village finally came into view, covered in mist, with a house standing alone at its edge. The house was small and nondescript, half-hidden by the encroaching forest.

Once, this house had been a home, but now the villagers kept their distance. They spoke in hushed tones about strange noises that came from within, about shadows that seemed to move even when nothing else did. To them, it was a place to be avoided.

Andrew approached the house, his mind unyielding, relying on his faith to guide him. He believed in the power of prayer and in the strength of good over evil. But this time, he faced something different.

This wasn't a restless spirit or a tormented soul. It was something older, deeply rooted in the house itself. It thrived on fear and pain, growing stronger in the quiet.

Jasper's gaze stayed fixed on Isaac, following every word about his father's encounter with Tashi. She had been a woman overwhelmed by grief and bitterness, her life filled with loss that had driven her toward dark paths.

Desperate for power to avenge her suffering, she turned to dark magic whose forces she summoned consumed her, making her a vessel for a demon that fed on misery. This demon grew stronger with every act of violence and despair.

The exorcism that night was harsh and unforgiving. The house bore the marks of a fierce struggle, its walls showing signs of the conflict that had taken place inside. Despite his efforts, Andrew did not survive the encounter.

He was exhausted, his body worn down. As the demon was expelled, it managed a final act of defiance. The strain proved fatal; Andrew suffered a heart attack. His body just couldn't take it anymore.

Chapter 2

A Son's Doubt

Jasper listened quietly, his uncle's story pressing heavily around him. His father had always been a figure of steady strength, someone who faced difficult things head-on.

But that strength had also led him to his death, leaving Jasper to carry the bear the ache of his father's absence. A constant ache, made sharper by the feeling that Andrew's devotion to his work had, in a way, chosen duty over family.

Jasper had struggled to reconcile his beliefs ever since. The prayers had stopped, and his trust in the God his father had served had slowly faded. There was no comfort in it for him anymore.

In the years since, Jasper had put his energy into a career of his own making, one that distanced him from the life his father led. Working as a child psychologist allowed him to help children process their fears, teaching them to find their own strength.

He'd seen firsthand how delicate young minds could be and how deeply they could be marked by trauma. It was a line of work that made sense to him—a way to offer relief and to feel some purpose, even if he hadn't inherited his father's convictions.

Isaac glanced at him, a flicker of understanding in his eyes. He hadn't expected Jasper to jump in, not without some sense of clarity about the past. He knew how different Jasper was from Andrew; he respected that Jasper had his own way of navigating life's darker paths.

Still, Isaac believed Jasper had inherited traits beyond the day-to-day skills of his profession. He had a resilience, even a calm in the face of fear, that Isaac thought might give him the perspective to help where others couldn't.

Rudra, who had been quiet through most of Isaac's recounting, shifted in his seat, his face tense but hopeful. "Jasper," he said finally, voice quiet, "I need to ask for your help. My daughter… She's a child who needs help. I don't know what's happening to her, but I know it's beyond what I can understand."

He held back a sigh, a mix of concern and hesitation building up. "I'm not sure why you're asking me, Rudra. This isn't what I do," he replied. "Maybe there's someone else, someone more familiar with these kinds of things."

Isaac stepped in, his voice calm but purposeful. "Jasper, I understand your hesitation, and I respect that. But no one else came to mind who I thought could help. I believe you've got a way of understanding people, especially children, that not many do. And maybe, that's exactly what's needed here. Just to see what's going on, and to help Rudra's daughter feel safe."

Jasper thought of the children he worked with, kids who dealt with fears and insecurities they couldn't always voice. He'd learned that even a listening ear or a calm presence could make all the difference. But this felt… different. The idea of going back, revisiting something his father died trying to resolve, brought up old resistance. He had seen where that kind of belief had led, and it wasn't somewhere he felt prepared to go again.

He looked down at the floor, trying to find the right words to express his hesitation. "Uncle, this doesn't make sense. I don't have the same connection my father had to that world. I can listen to Rudra, try to see what's there, but that's all I can offer."

Isaac nodded, a gentle understanding in his eyes. "That's all we're asking. Just listen and maybe look into it. We don't know what's happening, and neither does Rudra. Maybe we'll find that it's something else entirely."

Jasper exhaled, his uncle's words settling over him in a different way now. He could do that much—simply hear Rudra's daughter out, see if his training could help with it. And if it was more, well, he could decide then.

The resentment Jasper had once felt toward his father's choices had faded over time, leaving a kind of quiet acceptance that their paths were never meant to be the same. Yet, even as he listened, he couldn't shake the doubt that any of this was as mysterious as Isaac or Rudra seemed to think. To Jasper, it sounded like a case where a child needed guidance more than anything else.

He looked at Rudra, whose worry was unmistakable. Jasper realized he could help kids with what they couldn't put into words, whether it was an ordinary fear or something more tangled. And for a young girl, there was no reason not to at least try.

"Alright," Jasper said. "Tell me what you can, and I'll see if there's anything I can do. I'll try to help her, understand what she's experiencing."

A look of relief passed between Isaac and Rudra, though Jasper sensed his uncle hoped for more. Isaac relayed the details of the events that had been troubling Rudra, refraining from leaping to conclusions. Jasper listened closely, trying to filter out the pieces that might simply be a scared child's imagination.

For now, it was just about meeting her and seeing where he could be of help. He wasn't here to play any particular role or follow in anyone's footsteps, only to see if he could make a difference. And, for the moment, that was enough.

Chapter 3

The Exorcism in Vagamon

Jasper sat in silence after he'd spoken, and the quiet seemed to thicken around them. Rudra looked visibly relieved, yet Jasper could sense the lingering tension between them that had been waiting, perhaps years, to be addressed.

Isaac's gaze softened, and for a moment, he seemed to study Jasper, as if searching for something he couldn't quite find in his nephew's eyes. The silence stretched, both of them holding onto unspoken thoughts. Finally, Isaac leaned forward, his voice a low murmur.

"You know, Jasper, your father faced this same battle," he said. "It's a darkness that doesn't let go easily."

Jasper's mind, despite himself, began to pull back to those days he had tried so hard to forget. The weight of his father's fate pressed in, and memories surfaced unbidden, too vivid to ignore.

He could see it all clearly, even after so many years: Vagamon, the secluded town on the edge of the forest, shrouded in mist. He could still feel the quiet dread that hung over the town that morning, how even the air had seemed to hold its breath, as if anticipating something he couldn't see.

Andrew, in his clerical robe, moved through the morning mist. It hung loosely on him, worn more for practicality than tradition. His face, usually calm, showed the strain of the work ahead in the slight furrow of his brow. Beside him stood young Father Daniel, gripped his crucifix tightly, his knuckles white. His unease was clear, but Andrew didn't say anything—there were no words that could make what was coming any easier.

They shared a quick glance, a silent acknowledgment before moving forward. The door pushed open with a reluctant creak, exposing a dim room. The air inside was stale and heavy, a sharp contrast to the cool morning outside. It felt as though the house itself was holding back, waiting for what was to come.

The room was sparse, but what caught their attention immediately was Tashi, the woman they were there to help. She sat in the center of the room, barely recognizable as human. Her eyes were hollow, dark voids that reflected nothing.

Her skin had a sickly, unnatural pallor. A low growl rumbled from deep within her, a sound that made the hair on the back of Daniel's neck stand on end.

Andrew stepped forward, his face set in a grim line as he began the exorcism. His voice was steady, though it carried the strain of someone who knew what was at stake. He invoked the name of Jesus, not as a mere formality but as a desperate plea for help. The room seemed to react to his words—The walls strained, the floorboards creaked, and the room grew colder. It was as if the house was fighting back, resisting the very act of purification.

Tashi's body twisted in ways that should have been impossible, her screams filling the room with a sound that was neither fully human nor animal. Andrew continued his chants, his voice rising above the chaos, but the effort was clearly taking a toll on him. His face was pale, and beads of sweat formed on his forehead, his breaths coming in short, sharp bursts. The malevolence in the room was tangible, pressing down on him, growing more intense with each passing moment.

Father Daniel, standing a few steps behind, could only watch in horror as the exorcism unfolded. He'd seen possessions before, but nothing like this. The air was so cold now that he could see his breath, his hands shaking more from fear than the chill. Andrew's voice, though strained, remained strong, each word an act of defiance against the entity that had taken hold of Tashi.

Then, without warning, Andrew stiffened. A sharp pain shot through his chest, and his hand instinctively flew to his heart. His voice faltered, the prayer slipping away as he gasped for breath. The room seemed to close in on him, the darkness pressing harder. Father Daniel's eyes widened in alarm as he saw the older priest stagger, his strength rapidly failing him.

Andrew collapsed to the floor, the crucifix slipping from his grasp. His face was contorted in pain, his lips moving in what might have been a final prayer, though no sound emerged. Father Daniel rushed forward,

For a moment, everything went quiet. The tension in the air faded as the demon left her body. She slumped forward, unmoving, her life slipping away in the same instant. The room, once filled with chaos, now felt strangely still. She and Andrew both lay there, motionless, the battle over.

The memory shifted abruptly, yanking Jasper back to the present. Uncle Isaac's voice grew faint as he finished his recounting of that day, the pain still fresh after all these years.

"Your father saved many lives," Isaac said, almost to himself. "But the evil in that place didn't die with her."

Jasper nodded slightly, his uncle's words settling in his mind. His father's sacrifice, something he had always known about but never fully understood, now took on a new, more somber meaning. It wasn't just about what Andrew had done, but about what had been left unfinished.

The scene in Jasper's mind shifted, this time to the day of Andrew's funeral. The rain was relentless, soaking everything it touched. The cemetery was filled with mourners, their faces somber as they stood around the freshly dug grave.

Church members, fellow pastors, and townsfolk who had known Andrew stood together, their heads bowed in silent respect as his body was lowered into the ground. The rain mixed with their tears, a poignant reminder of the sorrow that filled the day.

Among them stood sixteen-year-old Jasper, his face a picture of raw grief. The loss of his father had hit him harder than he could have imagined, and it showed in every aspect of his demeanor. His hands trembled as he clutched a worn Bible, its leather cover slick with rain. His eyes, red and swollen from crying, kept shifting between the Bible and the grave, as if looking for some sign, some meaning in what had happened.

But there was no comfort to be found. In a moment of overwhelming emotion, Jasper let the Bible slip from his fingers. It fell to the ground, landing in the mud with a soft thud that was quickly drowned out by the sound of the storm.

It was a small, almost insignificant act, but for Jasper, it was symbolic—a sign of his internal struggle, his inability to reconcile his father's death with the faith that had always been a part of their lives.

That moment marked the end of Jasper's belief. He couldn't understand how his father, who had spent his life serving God, had been left to die in the process. If God couldn't protect his own, what was the point? From that day on, Jasper slowly let go of the faith he'd grown up with, feeling more disconnected with each passing year.

The rain poured, blurring the lines between the living and the dead, between what was real and what wasn't. It was as if the storm was a physical manifestation of Jasper's inner turmoil, a young man grappling with a loss that he couldn't fully understand, let alone accept.

As the other mourners began to disperse, Jasper remained by the grave. The rain soaked through his clothes, but he barely noticed.

Standing alone by the grave, Jasper didn't feel comforted by the faith his father had held so tightly. In fact, it felt distant, like something he couldn't quite reach. But there was no denying that his life had changed.

Chapter 4

Arrival on Cursed Land

12 Years After Andrew's Death

The flight had been uneventful, but as Rudra and his daughter Arvi walked through the small airport terminal, he found himself taking in the unfamiliar surroundings with quiet curiosity. Vagamon's remoteness was evident, and the air carried a kind of stillness he wasn't used to.

A police officer stood waiting for them at the exit, his uniform neat, his manner friendly. He greeted them with a nod and reached for their bags as they approached.

"Welcome, Rudra," the man said. "I'm Officer Koshy from the Vagamon station. I'll be taking you to your new place. Good to finally meet our new transfer." His voice was open, though there was a certain reserve, perhaps just politeness, that Rudra noticed.

"Thanks," Rudra replied, giving him a brief nod. He glanced at Arvi, who stayed silent, calmly observing everything around her. She had been thoughtful and a bit withdrawn these past few weeks, which he chalked up to the move and the changes ahead.

They followed Officer Koshy to the jeep, loading their bags into the back before climbing in. The drive to the new house was longer than Rudra had expected, and the silence in the car was broken only by the occasional hum of the engine and the soft rustling of the forest outside. Arvi sat with her face pressed against the window, watching the trees go by. She hadn't said much since leaving the city, and her silence wasn't out of place.

As the jeep bumped along the uneven road, Officer Koshy glanced at Rudra through the rearview mirror. “Not much has changed here,” he said, trying to fill the silence. “Still quiet, still peaceful.”

Rudra gave a brief nod, not really paying much attention to Officer Koshy’s attempt at conversation. "Peaceful" wasn’t something he thought about too much. He wasn’t looking for anything deeper in the air or the place itself. All he wanted was to settle in and spend some quiet time with Arvi, away from the rush of their old life.

After a while, the trees began to thin out, and Rudra saw the outline of their new house in the distance. It was still under construction, with scaffolding surrounding the half-built walls and workers moving about the site. The land it stood on was vast, the house sitting alone at the edge of the forest It was a fresh beginning, away from the chaos, though the quiet was harder to adjust to.

As they neared the house, Rudra glanced back at Arvi. She had turned her head from the window, her gaze now fixed on the tree line in the distance. The trees were thick and still, their dark shapes unmoving, even as the wind blew through the open car windows.

“We’re here,” Officer Koshy said, pulling the jeep to a stop in front of the house. He climbed out and started unloading their bags, but Rudra hesitated, his eyes fixed on the half-built structure. It was larger than he had imagined, almost too large for just the two of them. But he had wanted to build something permanent, something that would feel like home—a real home, far from the memories they had left behind.

Arvi stepped out of the jeep first, her small frame dwarfed by the scaffolding and construction equipment around her. She didn’t say anything, just stood there, looking at the house and then, once again, at the forest. There was the way she stared at it that seemed normal to Rudra, maybe even a little excited, as though she was lost in her own thoughts like any curious child.

This is home now,” Rudra said warmly, a reassuring smile lighting up his face. The words felt natural, a reminder as much for himself as for Arvi. He looked over at her, catching a faint, curious smile as she took in the surroundings, the start of something new.

Officer Koshy stood beside Rudra as they both looked over the house. "It's coming along well," the officer noted casually, his gaze steady on the structure. "Won't be too long before it's finished."

Rudra nodded, a small smile forming. He reminded himself that this move was about starting fresh, building a place where he and Arvi could settle in and feel at home. Looking at the house, half-framed by the trees and hills beyond, he felt a sense of anticipation grow.

The surroundings might be unfamiliar, but he found himself looking forward to the change, ready to make this place their own. He wasn't the type to dwell on unnecessary details, and his focus remained on getting things set up for them. The dense forest nearby barely registered as a concern.

Koshy hesitated for a moment, then cleared his throat. "You've picked a quiet spot here, sir. Away from the busier parts of town, plenty of space. But…" He paused before adding, "Locals say this land has a bit of history."

Rudra glanced at him, mildly curious. "History?"

Koshy shrugged slightly. "Folks around here say the land's cursed. Stories about strange things happening, accidents, people disappearing."

He raised an eyebrow. "Cursed? That's just superstition, isn't it?"

Koshy chuckled lightly, but there was a trace of unease in his voice. "Yeah, mostly. Small towns tend to have their share of stories. But you'll hear about it now and then."

Rudra kept his expression neutral, not giving it much thought. "I'm not sure I believe in that sort of thing. Curses, superstitions... people will always have something to say. Nothing to be concerned about."

He nodded. "Fair enough. Just thought I'd mention it, in case you heard anything. I'm sure you'll be fine out here."

Rudra shrugged slightly, his mind already moving on. "Let them talk. It's just land, like anywhere else. We'll settle in without any issues."

As Koshy nodded in agreement, Arvi remained standing off to the side, her gaze drifting toward the forest. Rudra glanced at her, noticing her quiet presence but not sensing anything out of the ordinary.

"Come on," he said gently, walking over to her and placing a hand on her shoulder. "Let's head inside."

Arvi was still standing a few feet away, staring at the forest again. Rudra walked over to her and placed a hand on her shoulder. "Let's go inside," he said softly. She didn't respond, but after a moment, she turned and followed him toward the house.

As they approached the front door, Rudra couldn't shake the feeling that was watching them, hidden within the trees. He glanced over his shoulder at the forest, but there was nothing there—just the same stillness that had greeted them when they arrived.

Officer Koshy lingered for a moment, looking like he wanted to say something else but deciding against it. "I'll check in with you in a few days," he said instead. "Let me know if you need anything."

"Thanks," Rudra replied, though his attention was momentarily pulled to the house and the view beyond. His thoughts wandered as he took in the unfamiliar surroundings, considering what this new place would hold for him and Arvi.

As Officer Koshy drove away, Rudra stood in front of the house, staring at the land that stretched out before him.

Rudra didn't care about curses or rumors. He had never believed in that kind of thing, and he wasn't about to start now. This was their home, and he was determined to make it work. No matter what the land had to say about it.

Chapter 5

A Price for Justice

2 Months Before

The sun was setting over Hyderabad, casting a golden glow over the city's chaotic streets. In his cramped office at the local police station, Rudra sat behind his desk, reviewing the files scattered before him. His back ached from hours of sitting, but his mind remained focused on the case at hand—an eve-teasing incident that had turned into a media circus.

A young woman from one of the city's prestigious colleges had filed a complaint. She had been harassed by a group of students, one of whom was the son of a prominent local politician. Rudra had dealt with cases like this before, but this one carried an added weight. The politician's son was known for getting away with things. His father's influence had shielded him from the consequences of his actions for far too long.

As Rudra flipped through the case notes, his thoughts drifted back to his own time as a young officer, fresh out of training. He had always believed in upholding the law without fear or favor, but over the years, he had learned that justice wasn't always straightforward.

Pressure came from all sides—politicians, businessmen, and sometimes even his own colleagues. Still, Rudra had managed to navigate these challenges, never once compromising his principles. He had earned a reputation for being tough, but fair. And now, that reputation was being tested.

A knock on the door broke his concentration.

"Come in," Rudra called, his eyes still on the file.

The door opened, and Officer Rajan, one of Rudra's most trusted subordinates, entered the room.

"Sir," Rajan began, hesitating for a moment. "We've arrested the Surender's son, just as you ordered. But... there's something you should know."

Rudra looked up, noting the unease in Rajan's voice. "What is it?"

"The politician's office called," Rajan said, his voice low. "They're furious. They want you to drop the charges and release the boy. Said it's just a misunderstanding."

Rudra leaned back in his chair, his jaw tightening. He had expected this. "And what did you tell them?"

"I told them it was your decision," Rajan replied, shifting nervously. "But, sir, they're threatening to go to the higher-ups. This could get messy."

Rudra nodded slowly, considering his options. He could drop the charges, avoid the political fallout, and move on. It would be the easier path. But every fiber of his being resisted the idea. The girl who had filed the complaint deserved justice, and Rudra wasn't the type to back down from doing what was right, no matter the consequences.

"Let them go to the higher-ups," Rudra said, his voice firm. "We're not dropping the charges. If the boy broke the law, he'll face the consequences, just like anyone else."

Rajan looked at him, admiration but concern mingling in his expression. "Understood, sir. I'll make sure everything is in order."

As Rajan left the room, Rudra returned to the file, but his thoughts were no longer on the details of the case. He knew what was coming. Standing up to a politician wasn't just about the boy in question—it was about challenging the system, a system that too often bent under the pull of money and influence. And Rudra knew that such challenges came with a price.

A few days later, the phone rang in Rudra's office, and this time, it wasn't just an irritated politician on the other end. It was his commanding officer, calling from headquarters.

"Rudra, we need to talk," the voice on the other end said with a faint but clear warning.

Rudra braced himself. "Yes, sir?"

"Look, I know you're a man of principle," the commanding officer began, "but you've stirred up quite the storm with this arrest. The politician's office has been calling non-stop, and now the higher-ups are involved. They want you to reconsider."

"With all due respect, sir, the law was broken," Rudra replied, keeping his voice steady. "I can't just let it slide because of who the boy's father is."

"I understand that," the commanding officer sighed, "but you need to think about the bigger picture here. You've got a promising career ahead of you, but if you keep clashing with certain people, it's going to cost you. You know how these things work. It's not just about right and wrong—it's about staying in the game long enough to make a real difference."

Rudra felt annoyed, his patience wearing thin. He had heard these arguments before—the idea that bending the rules occasionally was necessary to survive in the system. But that logic had never sat well with him.

"I became a police officer to uphold the law," he said firmly. "If I can't stay true to that, what's the point?"

There was a long pause on the other end of the line. When the commanding officer finally spoke, carrying a hint of sympathy.

"I get it, Rudra. I do. But I've been in this game a lot longer than you, and I'm telling you—pick your battles. This one isn't worth it."

"I'll decide which battles are worth it," he replied, his voice hardening. "If the boy's guilty, he'll face the consequences."

The line went silent for a moment before the commanding officer spoke again, his voice resigned. "Alright. But don't say I didn't warn you."

Two weeks later, the transfer orders came. He wasn't surprised when he opened the envelope, reading the official notice that he was being reassigned to a remote hill station. It wasn't framed as a punishment, of course—it never was. The letter praised his dedication and hard work, commending him for his service. But the message was clear: his refusal to back down had made him too much of a liability.

As he packed up his office, he reflected on his career. He had always known that standing up for what was right would come at a cost, but he hadn't expected to be pushed so far from the city, from the frontline of the action.

The hill station, Vagamon, was over 1000 kilometers away from where he had made a name for himself. It was a quiet place, with a crime rate so low it barely registered. A place for officers nearing retirement, not for someone like him, still in his prime.

His thoughts were interrupted by a knock at the door. It was Officer Rajan, carrying a small box of Rudra's belongings.

"You're really going through with it, huh?" Rajan asked, placing the box on the desk.

"Not much choice," he replied with a shrug. "Orders are orders."

Rajan hesitated, then spoke. "Sir, I know you did the right thing. Not everyone would've had the guts to stand up to them like you did."

Rudra gave a small nod. "Thanks, Rajan. But doing the right thing doesn't always come with a reward. Sometimes it's just about knowing you didn't compromise."

Rajan paused, glancing down before continuing. "You're not the only one they've been moving around. Ever since things started getting tense, a lot of good officers have been transferred—anyone who didn't toe the line. The city's political mess is getting to everyone. But…" He hesitated, then pressed on. "Arvi's been caught in the middle of this too, sir. She needs you, now more than ever."

Rudra looked at him, not saying anything, but Rajan continued.

"I know the city is where the action is, and you've always been on the front lines. But maybe this transfer is an opportunity. Arvi's growing up, and it hasn't been easy for her without her mother. This new place… it might give you the chance to spend time with her, away from all this craziness. It could be good for both of you."

Rudra didn't reply immediately. He hadn't thought about it in that way, but his words struck a chord. Arvi had never complained, never voiced any resentment over the constant changes or the long hours he worked, but he knew it had taken a toll. She was at an age where stability mattered, and maybe Rajan was right—maybe this quiet hill station would give them both some much-needed peace.

"You might be right," Rudra said quietly. "Maybe this is what we need."

Rajan smiled, relieved that he was considering it. "No one's going to fault you for taking this time, sir. Just make the most of it."

Two months later, Rudra stood outside the house that would be his new home in Vagamon. The air was cooler here, the landscape serene and untouched by the chaos of the city. It was peaceful, but that peace came with a sense of isolation.

It was quiet, too quiet. The kind of quiet that makes you feel like you've been forgotten by the world.

But he wasn't here to dwell on the past. He was here to do his job, even if that job was now far removed from the bustling streets of Hyderabad. And no matter how remote this place was, no matter how low the crime rate, he would continue to stand by the principles that had guided him this far.

Chapter 6

The Beginning

Rudra stood in the living room, surrounded by half-opened boxes. His hands carefully unwrapped dishes and placed them in the kitchen cupboards. The house, though livable, still felt incomplete. Furniture was scattered around, some rooms still needed final touches, but it was slowly coming together. He felt at peace, the stillness of the place helping him move on from the past.

"Dad! This place is so big!" Arvi's voice echoed from upstairs, full of excitement as she explored every corner of their new home.

"Don't get lost up there!" he called back, smiling to himself. The excitement in her voice made him feel like they'd made the right decision moving here. It had been a long process—leaving behind the noise and chaos of Hyderabad—but it felt like they had finally found a place to breathe.

After finishing with the dishes, he wiped his hands on a towel and glanced out the back window. Beyond the kitchen lay an overgrown garden, wild and untouched for years. It looked like it had potential, though—a place where he and Arvi could spend their evenings. With some effort, they could plant trees, put in some flowers, maybe even create a cozy spot to relax.

"Dad! I'm going outside to check out the garden!" she shouted as she darted past him and out the back door.

"Don't go too far!" he said, though he wasn't particularly worried. The house stood on the edge of the forest, isolated from any main roads. He liked the quiet, the sense of being removed from everything.

Outside, Arvi skipped across the backyard, her eyes lighting up as she took in the wild garden. The overgrown grass and weeds didn't deter her—she could already picture where they could plant flowers, maybe even a vegetable patch. Her mind buzzed with excitement.

She ran back toward the house and shouted through the window, "Dad! We can plant all sorts of trees here!"

Rudra smiled and nodded, watching her enthusiasm. "Sure, but let's finish unpacking first."

Just as he was about to head back to work, there was a knock at the front door. Frowning slightly, Rudra wiped his hands and walked to the door. They hadn't expected any visitors. When he opened it, he was greeted by a man with a friendly smile standing on the porch.

"Hello! I'm Isaac. I live just down the road," the man said, extending his hand. He looked like a local, dressed simply, with salt-and-pepper hair.

"Rudra," he replied, shaking Isaac's hand. "Nice to meet you."

"I saw you and your daughter moving in," Isaac said, glancing around the hallway filled with unpacked boxes. "Figured I'd come by and introduce myself. See how you're settling in."

"Thanks," Rudra replied, still somewhat guarded but polite. "We're managing, still got a lot to do."

Isaac leaned slightly against the doorframe. "This is a quiet place, but it's got history. Some say the land around here has been through… things."

Rudra raised an eyebrow. "Or so I've heard, but what kind of things?"

Isaac gave a small shrug. "You know how it is with old places. People talk. Some call it cursed land, say it's best to leave certain parts of it undisturbed."

Rudra crossed his arms. "I don't give much thought to it. I'm just here to get things set up and spend time with my daughter."

Isaac smiled warmly. "I hear you. I've lived here a long time, and I've heard all sorts of stories. It's a huge place, though, quiet. You'll get used to it."

As Rudra turned to check on Arvi, he remembered to ask, “By the way, what do you do around here?”

Isaac responded. “I’m a pastor. I help out in the community, offer spiritual guidance, that sort of thing. If you ever need anything—advice, help settling in, or just someone to talk to—feel free to reach out.”

“Appreciate that,” Rudra said with a nod. “Nice meeting you.”

“Likewise,” Isaac replied. “Good luck with the unpacking.”

Rudra closed the door as Isaac left, feeling a bit more at ease knowing they had a neighbor close by. But his thoughts quickly shifted back to Arvi and the garden, where she was planning their next steps; the sounds coming from there suggested she might already be at work.

Chapter 7

Whispers Beneath the Soil

The next evening, the sun hung low in the sky as Arvi made her way back to the garden to finish up her task. The air was warm, and the light breeze carried the scent of earth and grass. After breakfast, she had convinced Rudra to let her start planning where they would plant trees, imagining what the garden could become.

She had a trowel in hand and was digging small holes here and there, envisioning the space filled with plants and flowers.

As she moved from one corner of the garden to the next, she found herself stepping on a spot that felt different from the rest of the ground. She paused, frowning slightly. The earth beneath her feet seemed softer, almost like it was sinking under her weight. It wasn't quite like the rest of the garden. There was something off, as if the ground held more gravity in this particular area, pulling her down ever so slightly.

She knelt down, running her fingers over the soil. The earth here felt different from the rest of the garden—softer, looser. It didn't seem right.

Driven by curiosity, Arvi began to dig, her fingers scooping away the soil. As she worked, the ground seemed to shift under her hands, like it was giving way to what was buried deep beneath. She dug deeper, focused on uncovering whatever lay hidden.

Then, suddenly, her hand struck a sharp edge.

"Ow!" she yelped, pulling back and noticing a small cut on her finger. A sharp object had grazed her, just enough to draw blood. She stared at the cut, watching a drop of her blood fall onto the soil.

For a moment, everything was still.

Then, without warning, the air around her grew colder. The trees rustled softly, and the earth beneath her feet trembled ever so slightly. Arvi's heart raced as she knelt there, frozen.

And then, she heard it—a faint whisper, carried in the wind.

You found me.

Arvi's eyes widened. She glanced around, but there was no one there. Her breathing grew uneven as worry set in. She scrambled to her feet, trying to shake off the strange feeling.

The whisper came again, louder this time.

You are mine.

She stumbled backward, her heart pounding in her chest. Something was wrong—very wrong. Her hand throbbed from the cut, and her mind raced, but she couldn't make sense of what was happening. The shadows around her seemed to deepen, and the air grew thick, as though the garden itself was alive.

"Arvi?" her father's voice suddenly broke through the night, calling from inside the house.

She blinked, snapping out of her daze. She quickly stood up, brushing the dirt off her hands and trying to steady her breathing. Whatever had just happened, she wasn't ready to explain it.

"Arvi?" Rudra called again, stepping out into the backyard.

"I'm here, Dad," she called back, her voice shakier than she had intended.

Rudra walked toward her, his face etched with concern. "What are you doing out here? It's getting dark."

"I… I was just checking the garden," she said, avoiding his gaze.

Rudra frowned but didn't push her. "Come on. Let's get inside."

Arvi nodded, glancing one last time at the spot she had been digging. The strange feeling remained, but she followed her father back into the house.

As they stepped inside, her finger continued to throb, the cut stinging more than it should have. She rubbed it absentmindedly, but the whisper she had heard outside still echoed in her mind.

You are mine.

Chapter 8

On The Way

The fan in Jasper's hall creaked softly overhead, its steady rhythm filling the quiet room. Rudra leaned back, eyes distant as he recounted the story to them. Then, suddenly, His phone rang, jolting them all back to the present. He glanced at the screen and quickly answered "yes?"

The voice on the other end was muffled, but Jasper could see his face tighten, his hand gripping the phone just a bit harder than before. He shifted uncomfortably in his seat, the air around them thickening with a tension none of them could ignore.

"Yes, Koshy?" his voice dropped, his brow furrowing. "What happened?"

There was silence as Koshy spoke, and then Rudra's face paled slightly. He nodded, listening intently, his expression hardening with each passing second.

"We're coming," he said finally. "Stay with her, don't leave her side. We'll be there as soon as we can." He lowered the phone, slipping it back into his pocket, his gaze dark and focused.

"What happened?" Isaac asked, his voice low but steady, though there was a trace of unease in his eyes.

"It's Arvi," Rudra replied, his voice heavy. "Koshy says something's wrong. He didn't go into detail but he sounded scared, just that we need to come back immediately. I hope she's okay."

Isaac nodded, his face set. "Then we leave now."

Jasper took a breath, processing the sudden shift. He'd heard only fragments of Rudra's story, but he could sense that the situation was unraveling quickly. Whatever was happening with Arvi, it seemed that time was of the essence.

"I'll grab a few things," Jasper said, standing up. The words came out more resolute than he'd expected, but he didn't question it. Something about the urgency of the moment compelled him to act, even if he didn't fully understand why.

He left the room and walked down the hall to his own room, grabbing a small bag and starting to pack essentials. His mind buzzed with questions, yet he found himself moving with a strange calmness, as if he'd been preparing for this all along.

A soft knock on the doorframe pulled him from his thoughts. He looked up to see his mother, Joyce, standing there with a quiet, knowing expression.

"You're going with them, then?" she asked gently, her eyes meeting his.

Jasper nodded, slinging the bag over his shoulder. "They clearly need all the help they can get. I don't know how much I can do, but I'll try."

Joyce stepped closer, resting a hand on his arm. "You don't seem too sure about this, Jasper," she said softly. "But maybe... maybe you're meant to go. To see this through."

Jasper looked at her. "I don't even fully understand what's going on, and I'm not sure how I fit into all of this."

She offered him a gentle smile. "Maybe so. But think of the girl, Jasper. Sometimes it's not about being prepared; it's about being there when someone needs you."

He took a slow breath, nodding. Joyce gave him an encouraging pat on the shoulder before stepping back, letting him head out the door with Isaac and Rudra waiting by the car.

They climbed into the vehicle in silence, Isaac taking the wheel, his usual calm presence grounding the rest of them. As they pulled out of the driveway, the sky was thick with mist, the streets empty in the dawn light. The road lay ahead of them, winding through the quiet landscape as they make their way, leaving Kochi behind.

For a while, no one spoke. The sound of the engine filled the silence, its steady hum breaking the quiet of the car. Jasper leaned back, glancing out the window, his mind whirring with thoughts of what lay ahead.

Eventually, Rudra broke the silence. His voice was low, almost reluctant, as he began to speak.

"I suppose I should explain what's been going on with Arvi after the day in the garden," he said, his gaze fixed on some point in the distance. "It's not easy to talk about, but… we need your help, you should know."

Jasper turned slightly, his attention sharpening as he listened.

"The cut on her hand. I thought it was just a minor thing, nothing unusual. I remember telling her she needed to be more careful. But then, after a few days, something about it seemed… off., Rudra continued.

Jasper tilted his head, curiosity flickering in his eyes. "Strange how?"

"It didn't heal," Rudra replied simply. "No swelling, no infection. It was like her body just… stopped trying to close it. Every time I looked, the wound was still there, fresh as if it had only just happened. I tended to it, changed the bandages, took her to a doctor even, but nothing helped. The wound stayed."

Isaac's gaze flickered toward the rear view mirror, watching Rudra with a cautious curiosity. "Did she feel anything different with it? Pain? Discomfort?"

Rudra shook his head. "No pain, at least not in the beginning. But then she started saying strange things, almost like she felt… I don't know how to put it… a heaviness in her hand. She said it was like it was pressing down on it, like an invisible weight."

Jasper's eyes narrowed, absorbing the detail. It was unsettling, yet the way he described it was plain, matter-of-fact—a tone that made the story feel disturbingly real.

"That's when I started to worry," Rudra continued. "I thought it might just be her imagination at first, some reaction to the wound that wouldn't heal. But then…" He paused, a shadow crossing his face. "Then she started to change."

Jasper felt a chill, and kept listening, his mind open. He had come this far, after all, and there was no turning back now.

"What do you mean by 'change'?" he asked quietly, the question careful but pressing.

Rudra hesitated, his gaze distant. "She grew quieter. Started spending more time alone, especially in the garden. She used to love the garden, but now she'd just sit there, barely moving, as if she was… listening to someone."

Isaac cleared his throat, glancing at Rudra. "And did you ever hear anything in the garden?"

Rudra shook his head, his expression one of quiet frustration. "No, but she seemed convinced there was… a presence. She didn't describe it, just said that she felt 'watched' or that something was lurking under the ground. I didn't understand it, but I could tell it troubled her."

Jasper's mind drifted through the pieces of what he was hearing, trying to form a clearer picture. This was not the typical story of a restless child; there was a strange undertone that he couldn't ignore.

"So you're saying the wound, her behavior… it all started around the same time?" he asked, seeking clarity.

"Yes," Rudra replied. "It's as if a change occurred in her the day she got that cut. It was subtle, but… unmistakable. And now it's escalated."

Isaac kept his eyes on the road, but his silence was contemplative, as though he were weighing every word Rudra had said. Jasper could sense that his uncle was processing the details just as he was, searching for some unseen connection.

As the road wound on, the mist grew denser, the trees flanking them on either side like silent witnesses. Jasper leaned back, his thoughts lingering on the story he'd just heard. He wasn't sure what to believe yet, but it seemed like typical behavior for a troubled child adjusting to a new environment, especially without a mother around.

Chapter 9

The Sleeper

The car hummed softly as it curved along the narrow road toward Vagamon, a mist settling over the hillside as the day broke. Rudra's voice held an even, steady cadence, but his words carried a depth that kept both Isaac and Jasper listening in rapt silence.

"After the wound, I thought maybe that would be the worst of it," Rudra began, his hands tightening subtly on his knees. "A wound that wouldn't heal was strange, yes, but nothing that we couldn't treat or monitor. It didn't strike me as more than an odd coincidence." He paused, glancing out at the road before he continued.

"But then, only a week after it appeared, I woke up early one morning to the sound of water running." His gaze turned distant, reliving that early dawn with a mix of confusion and apprehension. "It was odd — the house was quiet, and Arvi never used the shower without asking me to help turn it on, especially not that early."

Jasper leaned forward slightly, watching Rudra's profile with quiet intensity. "So you assumed she was up?" he asked, though his tone implied he understood Rudra's confusion.

"I did. At first, I thought she must have woken up before me and decided to take a shower on her own." Rudra's face tightened with a slight frown. "But when I went to her room, the door was partially open, and I could see her shadow behind the shower curtain. That's when I started to worry."

The others were silent, allowing him to continue without prompting. He swallowed, the memory clearly bringing back feelings he hadn't quite reconciled.

"I called her name a few times, but there was no answer. I stepped closer, expecting to hear her voice, but it was dead silent apart from the water. So I reached in to turn it off, and that's when I saw her." Rudra's voice held a careful control, though his words hinted at a deeper disturbance. "She was lying in the tub, asleep — or at least it looked like she was asleep."

Isaac glanced at him, his face a blend of sympathy and thoughtfulness. "Did she look like she was… resting?"

Rudra shook his head, his voice thoughtful. "Not exactly. Her eyes were partially open, unfocused, staring, but there was nothing there." He ran a hand over his face, trying to find the right words. "Her body was relaxed, almost like she'd fallen asleep by accident, but it was… unnatural somehow. Like she was caught between being awake and somewhere else entirely."

Jasper felt a faint chill ripple through him, but he kept his gaze steady on Rudra, taking in every detail. "Did she respond at all when you called her?"

Rudra shook his head again, being frustrated at his inability to make sense of it. "I tried everything. Shaking her shoulder, speaking louder, even splashing a little water on her face. Nothing worked."

Isaac's gaze now remained fixed on the road, but Jasper could sense he was just as focused as he was. The way Rudra spoke of his daughter's unresponsiveness felt unnerving.

"And then?" Jasper pressed gently, encouraging him to continue.

Rudra took a deep breath, his voice softening as he remembered the moment she finally came around. "Eventually, she blinked, her expression shifting just enough to let me know she was… back, if that makes sense. But when she looked at me, it was as though she didn't recognize me, even just for a split second. Her eyes were red, almost bloodshot, and she looked… hollow. Like she'd been somewhere else."

"She held onto my arm, saying she was tired, too tired to stand, and I could feel her tremble as she leaned on me. I lifted her out of the tub, dried her off, and brought her back to bed. She didn't speak much after that, just lay there, barely moving. When I touched her forehead, she was burning with fever."

Isaac's brow creased as he absorbed the details. "Did you call the doctor then?"

Rudra nodded, his expression tight. I did. He came over, checked her over, and recommended monitoring her overnight to make sure the fever didn't worsen. He said it could be a reaction to the environment change. But in my gut, I felt it wasn't just a fever." He took a breath. "She was quiet all that day, barely moved from her bed. It was as though whatever had happened in the bathroom had drained her, left her empty. I didn't sleep much that night."

Jasper could see the toll it had taken on him. Rudra's face was weary, his eyes showing the strain of recounting the memory.

He continued, his voice almost a murmur as if speaking to himself. "The fever came back in the middle of the night. I heard her crying from the hallway, rushed in, and found her sitting up, trembling, her skin practically burning to the touch." He looked down at his hands, reliving the moment. "I didn't know what to do. I held her, tried to soothe her, but her eyes…" His voice faltered, and he swallowed, regaining his composure. "Her eyes looked through me, as if I wasn't even there."

"And then, when I finally laid her down, she looked at me, her hand reaching out as if to hold on… but her hand felt like a coal, burning hot. I almost pulled away, but I couldn't. She clung to me, her grip strong despite her weakness. I called the doctor, and he came and this time gave her a mild sedative, telling me to monitor her and bring her in if her condition didn't improve by morning."

Isaac's gaze remained steady, a silent support as Rudra shared his ordeal.

"The next day, she was back to herself," Rudra said quietly. "The fever gone, her energy returned. The doctor said it was likely exhaustion, some kind of reaction, but I didn't believe it. I couldn't shake the feeling that wasn't it." He hesitated. "Something… unnatural."

Jasper listened, his mind carefully considering what Rudra had said. He had dealt with many children experiencing stress or disruptions, but this situation didn't seem to go beyond what could be explained by a change in environment or routine. Still, there was an unease in the air he couldn't entirely ignore. The mist had thickened, cloaking the trees in a shroud of gray as they approached Vagamon, the landscape silent and watchful.

Chapter 10

Hunger Unbound

Eventually, Rudra spoke again, his voice low and careful.

"After the bathtub incident, I thought I could manage it —sleepwalking, maybe stress, or just the confusion of growing up. But things changed that very night. I was trying to get some rest when I started hearing noises coming from downstairs. At first, I ignored them, assuming it was just the fridge or some normal sound of the house settling in the night. But then… it grew louder."

"I woke up to some faint sounds coming from downstairs. At first, I thought it might be the fridge, but something about it felt off.". So, I got up, went down the stairs, and made my way into the kitchen."

Isaac, from the driver's seat, glanced back briefly, his steady gaze encouraging Rudra to continue.

"As I entered, the kitchen seemed unusually cold, almost as if it had been sealed off from the warmth of the house. And then I saw her."

"Arvi stood in front of the open fridge, the dim light outlining her small frame. She was hunched over, her hands gripping the shelves as she ate raw chicken straight from the package. I froze for a moment, unsure of what I was seeing. She wasn't just eating—she was tearing into it with an unsettling urgency, like someone driven by more than simple hunger."

"I rushed over to her, grabbed her arm and pulled her away from the fridge. I shook her, trying to wake her up, to make sense of what was happening. But when she looked at me, it was like she wasn't fully there. It was as though she hadn't realized what she was doing."

Jasper sat this in silence, the picture of the girl's odd behavior unsettling but clearly laid out.

"She paused, still holding the meat. Her face was expressionless, her eyes blank and bloodshot, not the usual look of a child surprised at being caught. And in a low voice, she simply said, 'Hungry, Dad.'"

"After that, she didn't walk back upstairs like normal. She crawled. She moved on all fours, slow and deliberate, like it was normal to her. I was too stunned to react at first, but then I followed."

He was scared, no doubt about it. Watching his daughter move in such an unnatural way, he felt a cold dread settle in the pit of his stomach. But he couldn't leave her alone—not when she was so distant, so unrecognizable. He stayed with her that night, sitting in the darkened room as she lay in bed, barely moving. Every now and then, she'd mumble softly to herself, her eyes vacant.

He couldn't explain what was happening, but he knew he had to be there. The fear gnawed at him, but he refused to leave her side. He told himself it was just exhaustion, that it would pass. But deep down, he wasn't so sure.

"The next morning, it was as though nothing had happened. She woke up normally, ate breakfast, and seemed completely herself. I wanted to believe it was an isolated incident, some strange sleepwalking episode that would never happen again." he continued.

"But the hunger…," he continued. "Over the following days, Arvi's appetite changed drastically. She was constantly hungry, asking for more food at every meal. She was eating well beyond what was normal for her age, yet she never seemed satisfied."

Isaac's gaze flicked up to the rearview mirror. "Did she show any signs of illness during this time?"

"The hunger didn't stop. It only grew stronger."

Jasper's eyes narrowed. "Stronger, how?"

"Her cravings grew more intense," Rudra added, choosing his words carefully. "Whenever she ate, she consumed unusually large amounts. It wasn't like regular hunger—she would devour food without stopping, as if she couldn't get enough."

Isaac spoke up, his tone thoughtful. "And the doctor—did he have any explanation for her symptoms?"

"No," Rudra replied. "He came over and ran a few more tests, checked her vitals. Her temperature was normal, and there was no sign of infection or malnutrition. When I mentioned the way, she was eating—the raw meat. He suggested it could be some kind of psychological response to stress or the move. He even mentioned the possibility of an underlying behavioral disorder."

Jasper glanced at Rudra, his expression serious. "But it didn't feel like that to you, did it?"

Rudra shook his head. "No, not at all. I knew my daughter, knew what was normal for her, and this… this was not normal. The cravings, the fever, the way she seemed to disappear into herself during these episodes—it all felt connected to something I couldn't see or understand."

Each man in the car seemed deep in thought, processing the strange series of events Rudra had recounted.

Jasper finally spoke, careful and direct. "Have you noticed any other changes in her behavior? Anything unusual beyond the hunger?"

Rudra considered this, his expression turning reflective. "There were moments, quiet moments, where I would catch her staring off into space, her gaze distant, like she was seeing something I couldn't. Sometimes she'd mumble, almost as if she were talking to herself. But when I asked her, she'd always deny it, saying she was just tired."

Isaac remained focused on the road, but Jasper could see the seriousness in his uncle's eyes. They were all heading into uncertain territory, drawn by the hope that they could help Arvi and uncover what was causing her behaviour.

"I just want my daughter back. I want her to be well, to be herself again. Whatever this is, whatever has taken hold of her… I need to understand it."

Chapter 11

The Call for Help

The dim interior of the car offered little comfort as the journey stretched on. Rudra sat forward in the backseat, his hands resting on his knees, his eyes fixed on the road ahead. What he had shared lingered heavily in the car, filling the silence between the three men.

Jasper finally broke the quiet. "So… why me? Why not someone local? Or someone who specializes in… whatever this is?"

He sighed, running a hand over his face. "Because this isn't normal. And believe me, I tried everything before I came to you."

Isaac glanced at Rudra in the rearview mirror but stayed silent, letting him speak at his own pace.

Rudra continued, his voice measured but tinged with frustration. "I didn't want to leave Arvi, not even for a moment. But after everything—the wound, the fever, her hunger—it felt like whatever was happening to her was bigger than anything I could handle alone. I went to doctors, specialists, even a priest in the town. No one had answers."

Jasper raised an eyebrow. "A priest?"

Rudra nodded. "Yes, but it wasn't like the movies. He came, said some prayers, and told me to keep faith. But nothing changed. Arvi stayed the same—or worse, she got more unpredictable."

Jasper absorbed this, his skepticism warring with the empathy he felt for Rudra. He didn't know much about Arvi yet, but he could see how deeply Rudra's worry had carved itself into him.

"That's when I called Isaac," Rudra said, glancing at the man in the driver's seat.

Isaac spoke quietly. "When Rudra explained what was happening, I told him that he couldn't handle it alone. It's not just about her symptoms—it's the house, the land. It's all connected."

Rudra added, "Isaac mentioned your name, Jasper. Said you'd distanced yourself from… well, from things like this. But he also told me you had a way of seeing through people, of understanding things that aren't always visible on the surface."

Jasper frowned. "And you thought that meant I could help?"

"Not just thought," Rudra said firmly. "I hoped. You're trained to deal with the human mind, right? Trauma, behavior, patterns. That's what this feels like—a kind of mental storm Arvi's trapped in. Maybe you can find a way to reach her."

Jasper leaned back, processing Rudra's words. He wasn't convinced, but he could feel the man's desperation. Still, he turned his attention to Isaac. "You told him it would take convincing?"

Isaac nodded, his gaze steady. "I know you, Jasper. I knew you wouldn't come if it was just me calling. But I thought if you heard it straight from Rudra, if you saw the fear in his eyes, you might reconsider."

Jasper crossed his arms, staring out the window at the trees blurring past. Isaac was right, of course. He wouldn't have agreed to this if it had been a casual invitation. But now, sitting in the car, he couldn't deny that Rudra's story had struck a chord in him.

Rudra interrupted his thoughts. "I didn't want to drag you into this, Jasper. But I couldn't let Arvi's condition go on like this. I needed someone who could see past what the doctors and priests couldn't."

Isaac added, "And someone who wouldn't run the moment things got complicated."

Jasper exhaled slowly. "Alright. Let's say I'm here now, and I'll listen. But I'm not promising anything beyond that."

Rudra nodded, grateful. "That's all I'm asking."

As the conversation faded, Jasper noticed a tension in Rudra's posture. "There's something else, isn't there?"

Rudra hesitated, glancing at Isaac for reassurance before speaking. "Before I left, I asked someone to stay with Arvi. I couldn't leave her alone—not after everything."

"Who?" Jasper asked, cautiously.

"A local officer," Rudra said. "Koshy. He's been… helpful since we moved here. He knows the area, and I thought he'd be a steady presence for Arvi."

Jasper tilted his head. "And you trust him?"

"Yes," Rudra said firmly. "I explained as much as I could without sounding crazy. Koshy didn't ask too many questions, but I could tell he understood that something's off. He's watching over her until we get back."

The memory of his conversation with Koshy from the previous day surfaced in Rudra's mind as the car hummed along the winding road.

"Koshy," Rudra had said, his voice steady despite the turmoil in his chest. "I need your help."

Koshy's response was measured, though Rudra could sense his curiosity. "What's going on, Rudra?"

"It's Arvi," Rudra said, pacing the living room. "I have to leave for a day, maybe two. I need someone to stay here with her."

Rudra hesitated. "Because it's not safe. I mean… not for her, not for anyone else. She's not herself, Koshy. She's been… acting strange."

"Have you thought about taking her with you?" Koshy asked.

Rudra exhaled, choosing his words carefully. "It's hard to explain. But I wouldn't ask you if it wasn't important. I just need you to stay here, keep an eye on her, and call me if anything feels wrong."

Koshy finally agreed, though Rudra could hear the doubt in his voice. "Alright, I'll stay. But Rudra, if this is more than what you're telling me, you need to be honest."

He hesitated for a moment before replying, his voice low. “I’ve been meaning to tell you, Koshy. Ever since we moved in, things haven’t been right with Arvi. At first, it was small things—her appetite, her unusual hunger... She started eating like she couldn’t get enough, and I thought it was just the stress of the move. But then, the fever came back and stayed, and she seemed distant, almost like she was... not herself. And then there was the way she started acting—crawling on all fours, not walking. It’s like she’s changed somehow. I can’t explain it, but it’s more than just a child adjusting to a new place.” He paused, his voice heavy with concern. “I don’t know what’s going on, but I have a feeling it’s not just a phase anymore.”

“Rudra, if this is really what’s happening, it’s not to be taken lightly. I’ve heard the stories, the rumors about this land, but I never thought it could affect someone like this. Whatever’s going on with Arvi, it’s beyond anything a doctor can fix. But you’re not alone in this. I’ll stay, keep an eye on her, and we’ll figure this out together.”

“Thank you,” Rudra promised. “Just… thank you, Koshy. I owe you.”

Koshy paused, his hand tightening around the phone as he processed Rudra’s words. He had lived in Vagamon long enough to know that new families didn’t just come and go without stirring up whispers, but this was different.

The moment he had heard Rudra’s voice on the other end of the line, asking for help, Koshy knew it wasn’t just the usual oddities of a small town. Something was wrong. He had seen Arvi when they first moved in—she had seemed like any other child, but there was a quietness in her eyes that unsettled him.

His instincts as a local told him there was more to this than just a child adjusting to a new place. Vagamon had a history, a history that was hard to shake, no matter how hard the new residents tried to blend in. And now, with Rudra’s call, Koshy couldn’t help but feel the heaviness of what was at stake. A new family, a new set of challenges—and now, an urgency he hadn’t expected.

Koshy had dealt with his share of local mysteries, but this felt different. He knew the land, the superstitions that clung to it like fog, but he never imagined they would touch someone like Rudra and his family. Still, his sense of duty overrode his doubts. This was a new family in need of help, and he wasn't about to turn his back on them. If something was wrong with Arvi, he'd be there. He had to be.

Chapter 12

The Garden's Whisper

He had arrived earlier that evening, finding Arvi already asleep upstairs. Rudra had mentioned that he and Isaac were heading to Kochi to seek further help.

Koshy, still trying to wrap his mind around everything, asked, "Who's Isaac?"

Rudra glanced over at Koshy, his expression weary. "Isaac's a pastor. He lives nearby, just down the road. He's been helping us settle in since we arrived. Checked in on us when we moved, made sure we had everything we needed."

He paused, looking toward the door as though ready to leave. "He's been a good neighbor, but more importantly, he has a nephew who's a child psychologist. Isaac thinks his nephew might be able to help Arvi, considering the... situation."

Koshy nodded, processing the information. "A psychologist? I guess it makes sense. Someone who understands kids might be able to help figure this out." His voice was neutral. He didn't show any sign that he thought there was more to it than that.

Rudra gave a small nod, his face tight with concern. "I hope so." With that, he turned toward the door.

Koshy sat in the dim living room, his hands resting on his knees, his gaze fixed on the staircase that led to Arvi's room. He had arrived earlier that evening, finding Arvi already asleep upstairs. Rudra had filled him in on the situation, his voice tense as he explained the strange events surrounding his daughter. He had told Koshy that he and Isaac were heading to Kochi to seek further help.

The clock ticked past midnight, its steady rhythm echoing through the stillness of the house. Koshy shifted uneasily in his seat, his gaze drawn once again to the staircase. He hesitated for a moment, his instincts pushing him to check on Arvi. He glanced at the stairs, weighing the decision.

Then, faintly at first, he heard it—a low humming sound, almost imperceptible. It seemed to drift through the house, growing louder with each passing second. His curiosity piqued, Koshy stood up and made his way upstairs.

When he reached the top, he saw that Arvi's door was ajar. He entered the room quietly, but found it empty. His eyes darted around, but she wasn't there. Turning, he moved toward the window and peered out into the garden, trying to make sense of the eerie humming sound that had drawn him upstairs.

There she was.

She stood in the middle of the garden, her small figure illuminated by the pale light of the moon. Her back was to the house, her arms hanging limply at her sides, her head tilted upward toward the sky. The humming came from her, rising and falling in a hypnotic cadence that made his skin crawl.

He made his way downstairs, towards the garden, cautiously stepping onto the porch. "Arvi?" he called, his voice low but firm.

She didn't respond, didn't move. The sound of the humming continued, uninterrupted.

"Arvi," he said again, louder this time. He took a hesitant step toward her, his eyes fixed on her still figure. "What are you doing out here?"

Her humming stopped abruptly, the silence that followed almost deafening. Slowly, she turned to face him, her movements stiff and unnatural.

The light from the moon caught her face. Her eyes were wide, unblinking. Her lips parted, and when she spoke, her voice was not her own.

"You shouldn't be here," she said, the words dragging like stones over gravel.

Koshy felt a chill race down his spine. "Arvi, come inside. It's late."

She didn't move. Instead, her gaze shifted, her head tilting slightly as if listening to something only she could hear. When she spoke again, her voice was even deeper, a guttural sound that didn't belong in the throat of a child.

"The soil remembers," she said. "It always remembers."

Koshy's chest tightened, his breath coming in shallow bursts. He took another step toward her, his hand outstretched. "Arvi, listen to me. Let's go back inside. Your dad will be here soon."

The corners of her mouth twitched, forming a smile that was anything but comforting. "He won't save you," she said, her voice dripping with malice. "No one can."

Koshy stopped in his tracks, his instincts screaming at him to turn back. But before he could act, Arvi's body jerked violently, her head snapping back as if pulled by an unseen force. She let out a guttural cry, her hands clawing at the air as her legs buckled beneath her.

"Arvi!" Koshy shouted, rushing to her side.

Her body convulsed on the ground, her limbs twisting at unnatural angles. Her eyes rolled back into her head, and a low, inhuman growl escaped her lips. Koshy dropped to his knees, his hands hovering over her trembling frame, unsure of what to do.

"Stay with me," he pleaded, his voice shaking.

Her body arched upward, her back lifting off the ground as if pulled by invisible strings. Then, just as suddenly, she collapsed, her body limp and unmoving.

His hands trembled as he reached for her, his fingers brushing against her forehead. Her skin was clammy, her breathing shallow. "Arvi," he whispered, his voice breaking.

Her eyes fluttered open, and for a moment, they were her own again—soft, frightened, and full of tears. She looked up at Koshy, her lips quivering.

"Help me," she whispered, her voice barely audible.

Koshy's heart clenched. "I will. I promise."

But before he could say more, her eyes rolled back again, and she went still.

Koshy sat frozen, the realization of what he had just witnessed hitting him all at once. His mind raced, trying to make sense of the impossible. He had seen fear, grief, and even death in his years as a police officer, but nothing like this. Nothing that defied logic so completely.

He pulled his phone from his pocket, his fingers shaking as he dialed Rudra's number. The line rang once, twice, before connecting.

Chapter 13
The Tether

As soon as the car came to a stop, Rudra stepped out, his urgency clear. Koshy was waiting by the front door, looking tired but tense.

"She's upstairs," Koshy said as Rudra approached. "Finally asleep, but it took some effort."

Rudra nodded and walked inside without a word. Jasper followed him, his focus on Arvi. He had listened to Isaac and Rudra on the drive but wasn't convinced by their explanations. To him, stress and fear were twisting the situation into something bigger than it was.

Isaac stayed back, his gaze shifting toward the garden.

"Where was she?" Isaac asked.

Koshy hesitated before nodding toward the yard. "I'll show you."

They walked across the damp grass, the smell of wet soil lingering in the air. Koshy led him to a spot near a large jackfruit tree, stopping by a patch of disturbed earth.

"She was standing here," Koshy said, pointing at the ground. "She said something strange, then collapsed."

Isaac crouched down, brushing his hand over the uneven soil. "What did she say?"

Koshy hesitated. "'The soil remembers. No one can save us.' That's what she said."

Isaac's fingers paused against the dirt. He glanced up at Koshy.

"It's been a long night," Koshy said. "I need to head home and get some rest. Will you be okay here?"

Isaac nodded. "I'll be fine. Go ahead."

Koshy left quietly, walking back toward the driveway.

Alone now, Isaac turned his attention to the soil again. Something caught his eye—a faint, pale shape near the edge of the patch. He brushed away some dirt, revealing a jagged piece of bone.

He picked it up and turned it over in his hand. The texture was brittle, the edges smooth—too smooth to be animal. Isaac set it aside and kept digging.

More fragments appeared, small and weathered. Then his hand struck something hard and metallic. He pulled it free, brushing away the dirt to reveal a tarnished cross. It was simple but deliberate, its presence unmistakable.

Isaac stared at the cross and the bones, his mind racing. Memories from fifteen years ago came flooding back—the fire, the rain, and Andrew's steady voice as they tried to stop what they couldn't contain.

"This is where we burned her," Isaac muttered.

He glanced at the soil again. They had believed the fire was enough to destroy her connection to the land, but the rain had stopped it before it could finish the job. They had left behind fragments—bone and relics that tethered her here.

The cut on Arvi's hand flashed in his mind. Her blood must have come into contact with the soil. That was the link, the spark that reawakened what they had tried to destroy.

Isaac stood slowly, brushing dirt from his hands. The realization sat heavy in his chest. The witch wasn't gone. She had been waiting.

Gripping the cross tightly, Isaac turned toward the house. This wasn't over. Arvi's life depended on what he did next.

Chapter 14

The Witch's Descent

Over two decades ago, the streets of Hyderabad, bustling with life during the day, grew eerily desolate at night. For Tashi, the darkness felt like both a refuge and a reminder of her isolation.

Once a mother who gave everything to raise her children, she now wandered the streets, abandoned and forgotten. She clung to memories of a life she could barely believe had been hers—a home, laughter, and love. All of it had crumbled when her grown children cast her aside, dismissing her as a burden.

The evenings were the worst. Hunger gnawed at her, and the cold pierced her thin saree. Her tears dried long before her sorrow did, leaving only a hollow ache. She begged during the day, hoping for enough coins to buy a meal, but the kindness of strangers was scarce.

One such night, as she sat near an abandoned stretch of road lined by the edges of a forest, her despair felt unbearable. Her thoughts spiraled darker than ever. Why had the world turned its back on her? Was there nothing left for her?

As her sobs quieted into exhaustion, a faint sound reached her—a slow, rhythmic clinking, almost metallic. Tashi looked up, startled. A figure emerged from the shadows, his silhouette towering against the dim moonlight.

He wore a black robe that swept the ground, adorned with what appeared to be necklaces of what looked like bones or skulls. His face was partially obscured, but his eyes glowed faintly, like embers.

"Lost, are we?" he asked, his voice deep and gravelly.

She didn't reply at first, unsure whether this man was real or a hallucination born of her despair. He stepped closer, and she drew back instinctively.

"I can see it," he continued. "The emptiness. The pain. Betrayal has a way of hollowing you out."

She froze, his words cutting too close to the truth. "Who are you?" she asked, her voice trembling.

"Someone who understands suffering," he said. "But more importantly, someone who knows how to overcome it."

She hesitated, then spoke in a rush, as if unburdening herself might offer some relief. She told him about her children's abandonment, her struggle to survive, and the gnawing loneliness that consumed her. The man listened silently, his head tilted slightly, as though weighing her words.

When she finished, he said, "Your problem is that you seek comfort from others. People will always fail you. Even those closest to you. If you want to survive, you need something that will never leave you. Something that will make you stronger."

"What... what do you mean?" Tashi asked.

The man crouched before her, his glowing eyes locking onto hers. "Power. The kind that doesn't fade. The kind that makes the world bow to you instead of casting you aside."

"I don't understand," she whispered.

"Black magic," he said, his voice almost reverent. "It's not just a tool—it's a companion. An energy that stays with you when everyone else leaves. Learn its ways, and you'll never feel powerless again."

Tashi recoiled instinctively. "Magic? That's... evil."

"Evil?" The man chuckled darkly. "Evil is what your children did to you. Evil is the way this world discards people like us. Magic is just a means to an end—a way to take back what was stolen from you."

She stared at him, her heart pounding. "You've lost everything," he said. "Why not gain something instead? I can show you the path, but the choice is yours."

For weeks, he stayed, teaching her his magic in the quiet, isolated woods. Each night, they practiced away from prying eyes. The rituals were strange. He made her carve symbols into the dirt—sharp, angular shapes he said would focus energy.

The chants were in a language she didn't understand, but he insisted she repeat them until the words came naturally. Sometimes she thought she felt the symbols or the chants working—a flicker of warmth in her hands, a shift in the still air—but she couldn't be sure.

He pushed her hard. If she hesitated, he made her start over. "You're not here to ask questions," he told her when she tried to make sense of what they were doing. "You're here to learn. Just follow what I show you."

She didn't feel in control. The rituals forced her to focus on emotions she'd tried to bury—anger, fear, grief. He told her these were necessary. "You can't push them away," he said. "They're fuel. If you want this to work, you use what you've got."

She followed his instructions, but nothing felt certain. The symbols, the chants, the rituals—it all felt unnatural, as if it belonged to someone else, not her. She wasn't even sure why she kept going. Maybe it was the faint hope that something would change. Or maybe it was because she didn't have anything else.

On his last night, he handed her a small, battered book. "Everything I've taught you is in here," he said. "The rest is up to you."

After he left, she sat alone in the clearing, staring at the book in her lap. The symbols carved into the dirt looked like meaningless scratches now. She opened the book once but closed it almost immediately. It felt too much, and she didn't trust herself to use it.

The days that followed blurred together. She thought about the rituals, the symbols, the promises he made. Had any of it been real? Would it make any difference? She didn't know. All she had were questions, and the answers felt as far away as ever.

One evening, she sat in her usual spot outside the temple. Her stomach growled with a hunger she had grown accustomed to, and her mind replayed the bitter memories of her children's rejection. A shadow fell over her, and she looked up to see a group of men standing there. Their faces were hard to make out, but their smiles put her on edge.

"You've been here too long, haven't you, amma?" one of them said, his tone deceptively kind. "Come with us. We'll get you some food and a place to rest."

The offer of food and shelter sounded tempting, but her instincts told her something was wrong. Too weak and hungry to think clearly, she hesitated for a moment before the men grabbed her arms and pulled her to her feet. She tried to resist, but her protests were drowned out by the noise of the street, and her strength was no match for theirs.

They shoved her into the back of a van with darkened windows. The air inside was stifling and smelled of sweat. Other women sat silently in the shadows, their faces showing exhaustion and fear. The van started moving, and the city she knew was quickly left behind.

The journey was disorienting. The van stopped only to switch vehicles or avoid checkpoints. Tashi tried to make sense of her surroundings, but the roads were unfamiliar, and the few words she overheard were in languages she didn't understand. All she could do was sit in silence, unsure of what was ahead.

They eventually arrived in Karnataka, where Tashi was thrust into a dimly lit warehouse packed with women of all ages. The traffickers barked orders, herding them like cattle. Her protests fell on deaf ears, and any resistance was met with brutal force. One slap was all it took to silence her, the sting lingering long after the blow.

For months, she lived as a prisoner. The traffickers made their intentions clear—they were commodities to be sold, nothing more. She witnessed women being dragged away, returning broken or sometimes not at all. Fear became a constant companion, but she clung to a small spark of defiance. She decided to

There after every night, she would close her eyes and think of the sorcerer's words. "Power," he had said. "The kind that doesn't fade." Her desperation to survive began to intertwine with a growing hunger for control. The thought of possessing something—anything—that could never be taken away from her became her anchor.

One evening, during a chaotic transfer, she saw her chance. The traffickers had loaded them into a truck, but their haste had left gaps in their vigilance. As the vehicle slowed to navigate a narrow road, she noticed the latch on the back door was loose. She hesitated for only a moment before seizing the opportunity.

She pushed the door open and jumped, landing hard on the uneven ground. Pain shot through her body, but she forced herself to run. Behind her, shouts erupted as the traffickers realized her escape. The sound of their pursuit spurred her forward, her bare feet pounding against the dirt road.

The forest swallowed her, its dense canopy shielding her from view but she didn't stop, even when her legs burned and her breath came in ragged gasps. She ran until she could no longer hear their voices, until her body gave out and she collapsed among the trees.

When she awoke, she found herself in a small hut. A kind farmer and his wife had discovered her near their field and brought her in. They offered her food and shelter, their compassion a rare glimmer of humanity in her otherwise bleak existence. For a few days, she rested, regaining some of her strength.

But she couldn't stay. The traffickers might still be looking for her, and she didn't want to risk the safety of the kind strangers who had helped her—the only people who had shown her compassion in years. More than that, the sorcerer's words had grown louder in her mind, an insistent whisper that refused to be ignored.

Power. The word consumed her thoughts as she journeyed southward, eventually crossing into Kerala.

By the time she reached, she was unrecognizable. Her eyes were sunken and hollow, her body a fragile shell of what it had been. Yet, within her burned an unrelenting determination. She remembered the teachings — the chants he had whispered to her, the symbols he had etched into the dirt, the sacred book she held close.

Desperation pushed Tashi to put his teachings to use. At night, she practiced in secret, drawing the symbols he had shown her and muttering the chants she had memorized. The air around her seemed to shift, small bursts of energy sparking in response. She managed to summon faint forces, barely bending them to her will before they slipped away. It was never enough.

While reading an old text, she found something that caught her attention: a ritual that promised immense power at a cost. The ritual involved opening a gateway to hell and inviting a demon to possess the practitioner. The warnings about irreversible consequences were clear, but Tashi didn't hesitate. She had nothing left to lose.

On a moonless night, she gathered everything the ritual required—blood, bones, ash—and carefully drew the symbols on the ground. Her voice shook as she began the chant, but she didn't stop.

The air grew heavy, the forest silent, and the ground began to shake. As the gateway opened, a figure appeared—a distorted, monstrous form with burning eyes.

"Who calls me?" the demon growled, its voice booming.

"I do," Tashi said, holding its gaze. "I want your power."

The demon studied her before letting out a deep, unsettling laugh. "Power comes at a cost. Do you understand what you're asking?"

"I do," she said without hesitation. "Take my soul if you need to. I just want the strength to never be abandoned again."

The demon's laughter stopped, replaced by a cold silence. "Very well," it said. "Your wish is granted." Its form dissolving into a dark mist that engulfed her. Pain ripped through her body, but with it came something else—power, raw and overwhelming, coursing through her veins.

Belial.

She knew the name from old stories—a demon of rebellion and control, one who thrived on power and domination. His voice echoed in her mind, calm but commanding. "You are my vessel now. Use this power with purpose. Together, we will take what the world has denied you."

When the ritual ended, she knew she was no longer the same. The demon's presence had merged with her, filling her with its strength. For the first time, she felt powerful. And with that power came clarity: she would make those who abandoned their mothers suffer, just as she had suffered.

The world had taken everything from her. Now, it was her turn to take everything back.

Chapter 15

Empire of Shadows

She stood in the dim light of her makeshift dwelling deep in the forest, her transformation complete. The demon's power was intoxicating and all-consuming. Yet, it wasn't aimless. The entity within her whispered promises of dominion, not just over her immediate tormentors but over the lost and broken who wandered the earth like shadows.

"You are my vessel," an omnipresent force that guided her. "But power without purpose is wasted. Build a following. Gather those who crave salvation, and they will serve me through you."

She did not hesitate. She knew her mission now wasn't just survival—it was conquest. Her anger toward her children, toward a society that discarded the vulnerable, became her driving force. She would take in those abandoned by the world, not to heal them, but to bend them to her will.

The first step was finding her disciples. She wandered through small villages and towns, careful to mask her true nature. She sought the young, the vulnerable—the outcasts who lived on the fringes of society.

"You've been hurt, haven't you?" she said. "They abandoned you, left you to deal with everything on your own. It doesn't have to be that way anymore."

To the lonely, she offered belonging. To the addicted, she promised freedom from pain. To the hopeless, a reason to keep going.

Her earliest followers were few—a boy abandoned by his relatives after his parents died, a young woman rejected by her family because of her mental illness, and a group of addicts living under a bridge, left with nowhere else to go. She didn't offer them food or shelter. She gave them something far more dangerous: the belief that she could take their pain away forever.

As her following grew, her teachings evolved. She wove a doctrine around the demon's influence, a twisted philosophy that mocked traditional faiths. "They told you to pray for salvation," she would say, her voice rising with conviction. "But where were they when you cried out for help? Where was their God when you were abandoned?"

Her message quickly spread among the disillusioned, drawing many people who felt angry and abandoned by a world that didn't seem to care about them. She spoke to their pain and frustration, offering them purpose and connection. To many, she became a mother figure, but her care came with a price: unwavering loyalty in exchange for the solace she provided.

Her rituals became central to her growing following. At first, they were simple—chants, prayers, and symbols drawn in ash and blood to summon the demon's presence. But as her influence grew, the rituals became darker. She began to demand acts of devotion that tied her followers not only to her but also to the demon.

Blood sacrifices became part of the initiation. She would prick her finger, letting a drop of blood fall into a chalice, and then require her followers to do the same. They would drink the mixture, a gesture she claimed sealed their bond. "This binds us together," she said, her voice firm. "Together, we are unbreakable."

The rituals also served a more sinister purpose. Each act strengthened the demon's hold over the physical world, allowing its influence to spread. She could feel its power grow with every sacrifice, every whispered prayer. She wasn't the only one bound to the demon—now her followers were tied to it too.

Her movement soon outgrew the forests. She began setting up gathering places in towns and cities, blending them into everyday life to avoid suspicion. Her followers, who now called her Mother, became recruiters, spreading her message to disillusioned youth. They focused on the vulnerable—addicts, runaways, and those abandoned by their families or society. Her promises of peace and purpose struck a chord, and her numbers grew rapidly.

Tashi's teachings were designed to dismantle traditional beliefs. "They taught you to fear demons," she would say during her gatherings. "But what have angels ever done for you? Did they come to your aid when you were cast aside? No. The power I offer isn't bound by their rules. It is yours to wield, yours to shape."

Her followers listened intently, seeing her as more than a leader. To them, she was a savior, someone who understood their pain and offered them hope.

As her influence grew, she began to draw attention. Authorities noticed the disappearances and the strange gatherings held in secret. But she stayed ahead of them. Her followers were loyal and protective, ensuring anyone who came too close to the truth was silenced—some through intimidation, others through more lethal means.

Investigators and informants often found themselves threatened, discredited, or, in extreme cases, disappeared without a trace. The loyalty of her followers made questioning her activities dangerous, and most people quickly learned to stay away.

Despite her growing empire, she remained restless. The demon's voice was always with her, urging her to grow, to bring more souls into its fold. "This is just the beginning," it whispered. "Build me an army, and the world will bow before us."

She was forging a new faith rooted in herself and the demon who fueled her power. She called it The Path of Shadows, a religion that promised relief from pain and eternal peace in return for absolute loyalty.

Her teachings pushed her followers further into her control. "The world has cast you aside," she would say. "No one understands your pain, but I do. Here, you belong. Here, you are seen."

She had completely transformed. The woman who once begged for scraps on the streets was gone. In her place was a leader who used the brokenness of others to strengthen the darkness within her.

As her following grew, so did the demon's power. Each soul she claimed brought it nearer to escaping its bonds and walking the earth once again. She knew this, but it didn't matter to her. Her pain had turned into her purpose.

Chapter 16

The Whispers in Vagamon

Lately, unease had spread through the town. People spoke quietly about strange events—shadows moving across fields, livestock vanishing, and young people falling sick without explanation. The name "Tashi" started to come up, spoken with a mix of fear and anger.

"She's a witch," an elderly shopkeeper murmured to a customer. "No good comes to those who speak her name aloud."

"Do you believe the stories?" a farmer asked his wife one night. She didn't answer, instead crossing herself and muttering a prayer under her breath.

In the center of the town stood a small stone church, its steeple worn down by years of monsoon rains. The church was run by Father Samuel, a man whose age and wisdom seemed etched into the lines of his face. His son, Daniel, a devoted young man in his early twenties, assisted him in tending to the small congregation.

The church had always been a refuge for the townsfolk, but even its walls couldn't keep out the growing fear spreading through Vagamon. He saw fewer people at Sunday services and noticed the uneasy looks shared by those who did come. Something was wrong, and it wasn't just superstition. Some had begun rebelling against her in quiet defiance, refusing to give in to the fear, but their resistance only seemed to fuel her wrath

One night, after locking the doors and preparing for his evening prayers, he stayed late in the church, hoping the solitude would help him gather his thoughts. The air felt unusually still, and as he walked through the dimly lit aisles, the usual sense of peace that the church offered was absent.

A cold draft swept through the hall, despite the windows being sealed tight. It sent a chill through him, and for a moment, he thought he heard soft voices, faint and unclear, coming from the altar.

Curious but uneasy, he made his way toward the source. As he approached the altar, the whispering became louder.

The candles on the altar flickered, their flames dancing wildly as if caught in a gust of wind. Then everything went still. The chill grew sharper, and Father Samuel felt an overwhelming presence surrounding him. His breath quickened, and he took a step back, his eyes scanning the room. He could no longer deny it: something was here—something that didn't belong.

The phone rang several times before a groggy voice answered. "Pastor Samuel?" Andrew said. A man he hadn't spoken to in a long time. "It's late. Is everything okay?"

"No," he said, his voice unsteady. Andrew sat up, now fully awake. "What do you mean? What's happening?"

"I'll explain everything when you get here, please hurry."

As the call ended, Samuel stood in the silence of the sacristy.

His thoughts were a whirlwind of doubt and fear. What had he just encountered? He didn't know, but he knew one thing for certain: the time had come to confront whatever darkness had taken root in Vagamon.

He called Andrew because he was the only one who could understand what was happening. They had first met during a diocesan retreat, where Andrew had shared his experiences dealing with forces beyond the ordinary. He knew there was no one better to protect the people of Vagamon.

When Andrew received the call, he didn't need to hear the details to know it was serious. Samuel was not the type to panic, let alone reach out for help unless the situation was dire. Andrew had dealt with enough in his line of work to sense when something was deeply wrong. He packed quickly, threw a bag together, and set out from Kochi. The two-hour drive to Vagamon felt like an eternity as his mind raced through the possibilities.

Years ago, he had been called to a remote parish where the people had lived quietly for generations. It wasn't the kind of place where dramatic events unfolded—at least, that's what he had thought.

When a series of strange incidents began to occur—a family vanishing without a trace, crops withering despite favorable conditions, livestock found mutilated—Andrew had chalked it up to rural superstitions. The townsfolk whispered about curses and dark rituals, but he urged them to trust in God and focus on their faith.

Then, came the night he couldn't forget. A young girl, no older than ten, stumbled into the church during evening prayers. Her clothes torn, skin streaked with dirt, and her eyes were filled with terror. "It's coming," she had whispered before collapsing in his arms. The events that followed still haunted him. The girl disappeared from her hospital bed later that night, and the parish burned to the ground a week later, leaving several dead and the survivors too afraid to rebuild.

He had stayed in that parish until it was clear he was no longer welcome. People didn't blame him outright, but he felt their stares, their silent judgment. They had looked to him for answers, for protection, and he had failed them. That failure had driven him away from the traditional ministry and into the work he now did—facing the darkness head-on, exorcising evil where he could, and learning to trust the instincts he had once ignored.

When Father Samuel called, it stirred memories Andrew had tried to bury. The fear in Samuel's voice was all too familiar, and this time, Andrew wouldn't wait.

Chapter 17

Echoes of the Witch

Father Samuel stood by the church door, waiting, exhausted and worried. He didn't say much at first, just nodded and led Andrew inside.

"Thank you for being here," he said, his voice low. "I didn't know who else to call."

Andrew gave a small nod. "You sounded shaken. Tell me what happened."

Without wasting any time, he led Andrew to the old quarters where he stayed. The building was small, tucked away behind the main church, with narrow, worn corridors. Inside the room, the air was thick with the scent of aged wood and candle wax. He sank into a chair, his shoulders slumped from both age and the heaviness of the events he had witnessed.

He sat across from him, calm but attentive. "Tell me everything, Father. What happened last night?"

He took a deep breath, his hands clasped tightly together. "I stayed late in the church to pray, like I often do after a day of services," he began. "At first, everything was quiet, as it always is. But then I heard whispers—low and faint at first, but they grew louder, surrounding me. It felt as if they were coming from the very walls."

He paused, his face pale. "And then I saw her."

"The Witch," Samuel said, his voice trembling slightly. "I've heard the stories about her—how she's grown more powerful, how she's building her following. People across the state speak her name in fear, saying she moves from town to town, spreading chaos, taking the vulnerable and the angry, and turning them into her disciples. And now, it seems, it's Vagamon she's after."

Andrew leaned forward, his expression focused. "What does she want here?"

"She wasn't after the church itself. To her, it's the people who gather here—their faith, their sense of community, their belief in something greater—that need to be torn apart. She sees me as the embodiment of everything she despises, the one who nurtures this unity she feels betrayed by."

"She called those who worship 'the false god' deluded fools, who deserved to suffer for clinging to a faith that failed her when she needed it most. Her anger wasn't just at God—it was at the people who find solace in Him, something she believes she was cruelly denied."

His brow furrowed. "Failed her?"

"She blames Him for her pain, for the suffering she endured when no one helped her. She's turned to something else now—a demon, I believe, Andrew."

Samuel's gaze dropped. "Because I stand for the church. I've told the people here to trust in Him, to believe that faith will protect them. I am a symbol of everything she hates. That I'm no better than the God she believes abandoned her."

Andrew leaned back, his eyes narrowing. "And what happened next?"

"She told me there's no redemption, not for her, not for anyone here. That it's time for everyone to pay."

His voice was steady but grim. "She's building power, to destroy the faith of this town, to feed off its fear and doubt. She'll only grow stronger."

Samuel's voice cracked as he asked, "What can we do?"

Andrew stood, his expression resolute. "We need to find out how she's tied to this place, how she's drawing strength from it. Once we sever that connection, we can weaken her. But we need to move quickly. She's not going to wait."

Andrew stood, his voice steady. “We start by understanding how she’s tied to this place. She’s feeding off the fear in this town and anchoring herself here. If we can sever that connection, we can stop her.”

He paused, his voice breaking slightly. "I’ve never felt fear like that in all my years.”

He nodded slowly, his mind processing the details. "You did the right thing. You should rest now, Father. You’ve been through a lot."

He looked at him, his tired eyes filled with a mix of gratitude and concern. "I will, but first, I want to make sure you’re settled. You’ll need your rest. Come, I’ll show you to your room."

He stood and motioned for him to follow. The old priest led him down another narrow hallway and opened a door at the end. Inside was a modest room, with a simple bed, a desk, and a small window that offered a view of the churchyard. It wasn’t much, but it would do.

"You can stay here," he said quietly. "I’ll bring you some food later, but for now, rest. We have much to do tomorrow."

Andrew stepped inside, taking a moment to survey the room before turning back to the priest. "Thank you, Father. I’ll rest, but we both know what’s at stake. We need to prepare."

He nodded somberly, then turned to leave, pausing at the door. "I’ll see you in the morning, Andrew. God be with you."

Chapter 18

Shadow's Grip

The events of the previous day stayed with him as he recalled what the old priest had said. The rumors, the strange occurrences, the whisperings of malevolent forces taking hold of Vagamon—it all seemed to be drawing him closer to the heart of the darkness.

Father Samuel's call had shaken him, but it was the inexplicable presence he had felt upon entering the church that night.

Determined to regain some sense of calm, Andrew decided to pray. His faith had always been his anchor, and in times of distress, it was the only thing that had brought him peace. He had been in situations like this before, where the spiritual forces of darkness sought to unnerve him. The unease that gripped him now felt like it was something more than just his own fear.

He moved toward the edge of the bed and knelt down. The small, simple room was dimly lit, the shadows stretched long across the walls by the flickering candle. He closed his eyes, took a deep breath, and placed his hands together.

"Our Father, who art in heaven, hallowed be Thy name," he murmured under his breath, focusing on the words. Each syllable, each prayer, was meant to ground him, to bring him closer to God, to shield him from the darkness that loomed just outside his perception.

A sudden noise broke the silence—a heavy object falling to the floor. The thud, though soft, echoed loudly in the stillness. Andrew's eyes opened, and he stood up quickly, his heart pounding as he tried to stay calm. On the floor by the desk lay a small wooden statue of the Virgin

Mary. It had fallen from its place, now staring up at him, almost as if it had been deliberately dropped.

He sighed quietly and bent down to pick up the statue. The cool wood felt smooth under his fingers as he placed it back on the desk. For a moment, he stood there, staring at it, unsure if his mind was playing tricks on him. Shaking his head, he returned to his kneeling position, trying to shake off the tension that crept up his spine. “Our Father, who art in heaven, hallowed be Thy name…” he whispered again, trying to find the peace he so desperately needed.

But before he could finish the prayer, another sound—a sharp crack—echoed through the room. A book, one of the heavy leather-bound ones from the shelf, had fallen. His eyes narrowed, and this time, there was no mistake. He hadn’t knocked the book off, and he certainly hadn’t heard any wind or shift in the air that would account for it.

He stood up slowly, turning to the book, his fingers tense as he picked it up. He placed it back on the shelf. He stood there for a moment, breathing deeply, the silence surrounding him again.

And then—again, another thud. This time, the candlestick. His brow furrowed as he stared at it. This felt… deliberate.

He chuckled softly to himself, trying to regain control. “Really? Is this what you’re going to do?” he muttered. With a small, almost cynical smile, he picked up the candlestick and, placing it back on the table, began to speak louder, determined to finish the prayer.

“Our Father, who art in heaven…” His voice wavered slightly but grew steadier with each passing word. “Hallowed be Thy name. Thy kingdom come, Thy will be done on earth as it is in heaven…” His voice was almost a whisper, but as he continued, the words felt more like a shield than a prayer.

As the prayer flowed from his lips, the noises started again, one by one. Things continued to fall. A small vase, a book from the shelf, the cross on the small altar.

Andrew’s voice grew louder, more insistent. “Our Father, who art in heaven… Hallowed be Thy name…”

As he turned back to the prayer, his eyes caught a shadow on the wall. It towered, taller than it should have been, its jagged outline shifting.

The flames roared as the figure stepped closer. The heat pressed against Andrew, heavy and suffocating, pinning him to the floor. He didn't move—not out of fear, but defiance.

The witch tilted her head, her eyes narrowing. "You're stubborn," she said, almost amused. "But stubbornness won't save you."

Andrew tightened his grip on the rosary. "Neither will hatred," he replied, his voice steady despite his trembling legs.

Andrew's breath caught as the figure grabbed the cross from the wall and ripped it down. Without hesitation, she threw it into the fire. The flames consumed it quickly, leaving behind only ash. Andrew didn't flinch, his focus locked on the figure at the edge of the firelight.

The air in the room grew heavier, and the temperature began to rise. Andrew's grip tightened on his rosary as he took a step forward. "By the authority of the Father, the Son, and the Holy Spirit, I command you to leave this place," he said.

Andrew took a deep breath, his knuckles white around the rosary. He turned as Father Samuel entered the room. "This isn't over," she hissed, her voice sharp and echoing. "You can't save them. You can't save yourself."

The shadow surged forward before Andrew could react. The room went dark as it passed through him, leaving him breathless and unsteady. He staggered back, gasping as silence returned.

When he looked up, she was gone. The fire burned steadily again, the frost melting into damp patches on the walls. Andrew stood there, his breath coming in short gasps as the adrenaline coursed through him.

Father Samuel entered the room cautiously, his face pale. "Andrew, are you alright? What happened?"

Andrew said, his voice low "she's not done."

Chapter 19

Crossing Into Darkness

The next morning, the sun had barely risen over Vagamon, casting long shadows across the narrow streets as Andrew and Isaac stood before the gathered elders of the church. As he looked into the faces of those who had spent their lives in service to God, Andrew felt a quiet strength settle over him.

He had told them of his encounter the previous night, of the shadow, of the desecration of the cross. He had spoken of the evil that had already taken root, in the very heart of the town. And now, it was time to face that evil head-on.

Each one of them had lived through countless trials, had seen the town go through seasons of suffering and peace, but none of them had ever faced something like this. The presence of evil in the town seemed no longer a rumor—it was real, and it needed to be eradicated.

Father Samuel, though older and frail, was the first to speak. "Andrew, we have prayed for wisdom in this matter. And while it is not for us to face this evil, we stand with you. Your faith gives us courage, and we will lend you ours."

Andrew nodded, grateful for their support. Still, a sense of unease remained. He had dealt with similar situations before, but this felt different. This wasn't just about an exorcism—it was about protecting the entire town.

Father Samuel looked to his left, where his son, Daniel, stood quietly, his face a mixture of determination and concern. "There is one more thing, Andrew," Samuel said, his eyes meeting Andrew's. "My son will accompany you."

Andrew turned to Daniel, surprised. "I admire your courage, but this is a dangerous task. I cannot ask you to—"

"I know what you're thinking," Daniel interrupted, his voice steady. "But my place is by your side. My father and I have been in this town for years, and we've seen many trials. I may not have your experience, but I believe I can be of help. Besides, this evil has taken root here. It's not just something we can pray away from the church—it must be destroyed at the source."

He looked into Daniel's eyes and saw nothing but determination. Despite his doubts, he knew that he was right. The source of the darkness, The Witch, needed to be confronted, and if it meant putting their faith to the test, so be it. "Then we go together," he said.

The elders blessed their mission, and Father Samuel presented a pouch containing holy oil, candles, and relics to guide and protect them.

Andrew accepted the pouch, the significance of the moment pressing heavily on him. He glanced at Samuel and hesitated, the words forming in his mind before he finally spoke. "Before we go, there's someone I need to call."

Samuel's brows furrowed. "Who?"

"My brother," Andrew said, his voice steady. "Isaac. He's a priest as well, and someone I've always trusted to stand with me in situations like this. He has a way of seeing things clearly, even when everything feels impossible. If we're going to face her, I need him here."

Samuel nodded slowly, his expression thoughtful. "A man like that could make all the difference. Call him. We'll wait."

Andrew stepped aside, pulling out his phone. He stared at the screen for a moment, as though contemplating the call. Then he dialed.

The line connected after two rings. "Andrew," Isaac said, his voice calm and familiar.

"I need your help," Andrew said without preamble.

There was a brief pause on the other end. "What's going on?"

Andrew broke it down—the witch's power spreading, the possession, and the town's fear worsening.

"Where are you?" Isaac asked, his tone sharp.

Vagamon. St. Thomas Church," Andrew replied

"I'll arrive soon," Isaac replied with certainty.

Andrew lowered the phone, exhaling deeply. He turned back to Samuel, his voice quieter now. "He should be here by evening."

Samuel gave a short nod, placing a hand on Andrew's shoulder. "Good. You'll need each other."

The three men made their way through the winding roads, heading toward the outskirts where Tashi's house lay. The road grew narrower as they approached the witch's residence. The houses on either side became more sparse, the landscape wilder, the air heavier.

The surroundings felt still, as though the land itself sensed the changes. Vagamon stayed peaceful, untouched by the encroaching darkness.

Tashi's house stood at the edge of the forest, a ramshackle structure that seemed out of place among the lush greenery that surrounded it. The building was old, its wooden walls weathered by years of neglect. The windows were small and covered in grime, offering no glimpse of what lay inside. A faint sense of foreboding hung in the air, and Andrew could feel the presence watching them.

"This is it," Andrew said quietly, his voice barely above a whisper. His instincts were on high alert, his senses heightened by the proximity of the evil he knew was waiting for them.

Isaac nodded, his face set. "We've come this far. We will finish it here."

Daniel, who had been quiet until then, stepped forward. "Let's do this."

Together, they crossed the threshold, the creaky door swinging open with an eerie groan. The house was dark, the only light coming from the dim daylight filtering through the grime-covered windows. The air inside was thick with dust, and the faint smell of herbs and something more sinister lingered in the corners. The walls were adorned with strange symbols, some drawn hastily, others etched into the wood as if carved by hands desperate for protection—or perhaps summoning something darker.

Andrew's grip tightened on the bag of holy items, and he reached for the small vial of blessed oil. "We need to find her," he muttered, more to himself than to Daniel or Isaac.

As they moved through the house, every creak of the floorboards, every rustle of the wind outside, felt amplified. The house was unsettlingly silent, as if it were waiting for something. They made their way to the small living room, where a fire still burned faintly in the hearth. There was no sign of Tashi—no sound, no movement. But Andrew knew she was near. The evil that had been plaguing the town radiated from this place.

"Do you feel it?" Daniel asked quietly, his voice low with unease.

Andrew nodded. "It's here. She's close. We have to be ready."

Chapter 20

The Confrontation

Just as Andrew finished speaking, the air in the room seemed to tighten, and a soft laugh echoed through the house—hollow and mocking. The sound seemed to come from everywhere, yet nowhere at all. It reverberated in the walls, in the floorboards, and in the very air around them. The hairs on the back of Andrew's neck stood on end, and the others felt it too. A deep chill crept over them, seeping into their bones. Tashi had arrived.

From the shadows, a figure emerged—tall, imposing, and draped in darkness. The dim light of the room barely touched her, but her presence seemed to consume the space, her very being distorting the air.

Tashi's skin was unnaturally pale, almost translucent, like a corpse that had been preserved in some dark ritual. Her long, raven-black hair cascaded down in waves, framing a face that was both beautiful and haunting. But it was her eyes that drew them in—glowing faintly with an unnatural light that burned with malice, as though every thought in her head was an unspoken curse.

Her lips twisted into a cruel, almost playful smile. It wasn't a smile of joy—it was a twisted reflection of her power, a manifestation of her deep satisfaction in the terror she had inflicted on Vagamon. A promise of more pain to come.

"Well, well, the priest and his faithful companion," Tashi said, her voice smooth, almost seductive, laced with an edge of cruel amusement. "You've come to try and stop me, haven't you? How quaint. But it is already too late. The darkness has already settled here. The land is mine now. All of it. And you? You are but fleeting, insignificant figures in a much larger game."

Andrew's heart pounded in his chest, but he refused to show fear. He had been here before. He had faced evil countless times, and each time, his strength had only grown greater. This was no different. He had come to end this. He had come to destroy this evil at its root.

He stepped forward, standing tall despite the growing darkness around him. "You have no power here, Tashi," Andrew declared, his voice unwavering. "This evil ends today. In the name of God, I command you to leave this place."

Tashi's laughter was immediate and cold, cutting through the air like a blade. The sound reverberated off the walls, rattling the small house with a power that felt almost physical. She let the laughter die down slowly, savoring the tension, before speaking again.

"You think you can stop me?" she mocked. "You think you, a mere priest, can undo what has already been set into motion? I've been here long enough to know how you operate. You rely on your faith, your rituals, your prayers. But I have something stronger than all of that. I have control. You are powerless against what I command."

Andrew's hands tightened around the small vial of holy oil he held. He didn't flinch. "Your power is a lie, Tashi," he said, his voice cutting through the heavy air. "The only thing that will leave this house today is you. This house, this land, this town, is no longer under your dominion."

With a steady hand, Andrew began to sprinkle the holy oil across the floor, marking the perimeter of the room. The oil glowed faintly as it hit the ground, a stark contrast to the shadows that clung to the walls. The smell of incense and the bitter scent of herbs seemed to intensify in the room, heavy with an undeniable sense of unease. But Andrew didn't hesitate. He continued his work, knowing that each drop of holy oil was a blow against the darkness.

Tashi stood motionless, watching him with cold amusement, as though the sight of him praying and performing his rituals was a source of great entertainment. "You think your pathetic little rituals will protect you?" she hissed. "Do you think your prayers can banish me?"

Andrew's gaze never left Tashi. "Your arrogance is your undoing. You may have power here, but it is not enough to break the light of God. This ends now."

Isaac stood by Andrew's side, his jaw tight, his grip firm on the cross that hung around his neck. As a priest, he carried the same faith as Andrew, but his role had always been one of steady support and quiet strength. He had stood with Andrew through many trials, but the presence of evil in this house was suffocating.

But Isaac knew one thing: they weren't helpless. No matter how strong Tashi's presence felt or how much she taunted them, their faith would hold. Together, they would see this through.

"We'll see who is truly powerless," Isaac muttered under his breath. His eyes never left Tashi, his body coiled like a spring, ready for whatever came next.

Behind them, Daniel stood firm, holding a small wooden cross in his hand. His hands trembled slightly. He wasn't the exorcist Andrew was, but he believed in the mission. He believed in the fight. And though he felt fear deep in his chest, he stood tall. He wasn't alone.

Tashi tilted her head, as if considering them all for a moment. Her smile deepened. "You are all fools. You come here with nothing but your words and your rituals. You think your god can stop me? I am beyond your reach. I have power you cannot comprehend. Power that will destroy you all."

She raised her hands, and the room seemed to tremble with her command. Shadows in the corners of the room seemed rised, twisting and writhing like living things. The walls seemed to pulse with the force of her presence.

Isaac's eyes narrowed. "We're not afraid of you," he spat, stepping closer to Andrew. "We've faced worse."

Tashi's eyes narrowed, the light in them flickering with something darker. "You haven't seen the worst of it yet."

Without warning, she lunged forward, her movements almost too fast to follow. Her fingers curled like claws, reaching for them. The house seemed to come alive around them, the walls groaning, the floorboards creaking as if the very structure was alive with her power.

But Andrew was ready. He stepped forward, holding up his hand in the shape of a blessing, his voice raising in prayer. "In the name of the Father, the Son, and the Holy Spirit, I command you to leave this place."

Tashi recoiled as if struck by an unseen force. The shadows that had stretched across the room began to flicker and fade, the oppressive weight of her presence lifting slightly.

"Leave this place now!" Andrew shouted, his voice a roar that echoed through the walls. The room trembled again, but this time, it was not the power of Tashi that shook the house—it was the power of Andrew's faith.

For a moment, there was a tense silence. The shadows that had filled the room began to recede, the darkness lifting from the corners of the room like fog retreating with the dawn. But then, with a scream that pierced the silence, Tashi collapsed to the ground, writhing in agony as the power that had bound her to this place began to break. Her body twisted and contorted as if it were being pulled in every direction at once.

Andrew, Isaac, and Daniel stepped back, but they didn't leave her side. They had come to end this. And now, it was almost over.

"You will not win," Tashi spat, her voice now hollow and unrecognizable. "You may drive me from this house, but you cannot stop me forever."

Andrew's heart pounded, but he held his ground. "We will stop you. And we will bury this evil once and for all."

Chapter 21

The Final Sacrifice

The air in the witch's house was suffocating, heavy with the dark energy that clung to every corner. The fire in the hearth flickered weakly, the only light in the otherwise pitch-black room. Shadows seemed to stretch and writhe, as if the darkness itself was alive, waiting to consume them.

Andrew, Isaac, and Daniel stood before Tashi's lifeless body, preparing to perform the exorcism. The witch's reign of terror was about to end, but none of them could have anticipated the cost.

Tashi's body lay motionless on the floor, but Andrew knew that she was far from defeated. Her spirit had already woven itself into the very fabric of the land, and it was not going to release its grip easily. They had come to destroy her, but they also had come to face a force greater than anything they had encountered before.

Andrew, standing in the center of the room, took a deep breath, his hands clasped around the vial of holy oil. He looked over at Isaac and Daniel, their faces grim but resolute. They had all prepared for this moment. It was the final step in freeing Vagamon from the evil that had taken root. But it would not be without sacrifice.

"This is it," Andrew said quietly, his voice steady but filled with purpose. "We must push through. Keep the faith. We will succeed."

Isaac, standing beside Andrew, nodded. He didn't speak, but the fire in his eyes showed that he understood the gravity of what they were about to do. Daniel, a few steps behind, gripped the small cross tightly, his knuckles white with the intensity of his focus.

Andrew stepped forward, raising the vial of holy oil high above his head. The words of the prayer, ancient and powerful, flowed from his lips. "In the name of the Father, the Son, and the Holy Spirit, I command you, spirit of evil, to leave this place. Be gone from this land. Your time here is over."

Tashi's body remained still, but the room around them began to tremble. The walls seemed to shift slightly as the air grew heavier. Shadows lengthened subtly, reaching toward them. A low voice echoed faintly from the corners of the room, its source unclear.

"You cannot stop me. You cannot break me," the voice hissed, vibrating through the floor and into their bones. "You are nothing. You are weak."

Andrew's grip tightened on the vial. "No. Your power is a lie. You are nothing."

But as the last word left his lips, Andrew felt a sudden sharp pain in his chest. His breath hitched, and for a moment, the world seemed to spin around him. His knees buckled beneath him, and he dropped to the floor with a gasp, clutching at his chest. Isaac's eyes widened in alarm as Andrew's face twisted in agony.

"Andrew!" Isaac shouted, rushing to his side. Daniel took a step back, panic flickering in his eyes.

But Andrew only shook his head weakly. "I'm... fine," he gasped. His voice was hoarse, strained. He tried to rise, but his body refused to cooperate. "Finish it... Daniel. You must finish it."

Isaac knelt beside him, panic creeping into his voice. "No, Andrew, we need to get you help—right now!"

Andrew's hand shot out, grabbing Isaac's wrist with surprising strength. "You must... burn her body," he managed to say, his voice barely a whisper. "Only then... will it be truly over."

Isaac's heart pounded in his chest, but there was no time to argue. He could feel the life draining from his brother's body with each passing second. There was no more time for prayers, no more time for rituals. The darkness was still pressing in on them, pushing against them with relentless force.

Isaac made a split-second decision. “I’ll get help,” he said, his voice trembling. “I’ll get you help, Andrew. Stay with me. Don’t give up.”

Andrew’s eyes, though clouded with pain, locked onto Isaac’s, a silent plea in them. “No,” he whispered, his voice growing weaker. “Go... now. Save the town. You... must burn her.”

Isaac’s chest tightened with the weight of his brother’s words, but there was no time to question them. He had to act. He had to do what Andrew asked. But in that moment, he felt like he was being torn in two—one part of him desperate to stay with his brother, to fight for him, but the other part knowing that this was Andrew’s final request, and that he couldn’t afford to fail.

“Stay with him,” Isaac said, looking to Daniel. “Do what needs to be done.”

Daniel, pale and wide-eyed, nodded quickly. He stepped forward, kneeling beside Andrew. “I won’t leave you. I won’t let you down, Andrew.”

Isaac hesitated for a brief moment, his heart breaking, but then he stood up. Without another word, he ran toward the door, rushing out into the night. The garden where they had planned to burn Tashi’s body was only a few steps away, and he would not waste any more time.

The Garden

Daniel stayed by Andrew’s side as the fire burned slowly, the smoke rising from the pyre that had been outside the house. The night air felt cold against his skin, but it was the warmth of the flames that kept the fear at bay. Andrew was slipping away, and with every breath, it felt as though the world was changing—becoming something heavier that Daniel didn’t know how to carry.

“Andrew... please hold on,” Daniel whispered, his voice hoarse with grief.

Andrew's eyes fluttered open once more, his strength fading with every passing second. His hand reached out weakly, touching Daniel’s arm. “Do what you must,” he said, his voice faint, as if coming from a distant place. “Burn her. The land is ours again.”

With those final words, Andrew's body relaxed, his hand falling to the ground. He was gone. His final act—his final sacrifice—had been made. The witch's body was still in the garden, the last remnants of her dark power waiting to be eradicated. And Daniel knew what he had to do.

The Burning

Daniel stood, his breath coming in shallow gasps. He had already set the pyre. The dry wood around Tashi's body had been gathered, and the holy oil had been spread across it. He could feel it all bearing down on him—Andrew's death, the witch's curse, and the responsibility of finishing what they had started.

With trembling hands, Daniel lit the match, striking it against the stone. The flame caught quickly, and in a moment, the pyre ignited. The flames licked at the air, crackling as they consumed Tashi's body. The witch, whose dark influence had poisoned Vagamon for so long, was finally being reduced to ash.

As the fire burned, Daniel stood back, watching in silence. There was no joy in the destruction of the body. There was no sense of victory. There was only the quiet, suffocating weight of loss.

And yet, deep inside, Daniel knew that Andrew had given everything to ensure the evil was gone. Now, it was his turn to shoulder both the grief and the responsibility.

Isaac's Return

Isaac returned later that night, his face a mixture of exhaustion and sorrow. He had gone to the nearest town, seeking help, but by the time he had returned, it was too late. Andrew was gone, and nothing could bring him back. He walked to the pyre, his heart heavy, and stood beside Daniel.

The two brothers had faced countless trials together. But this—the loss of Andrew—was a trial neither of them had been prepared for.

But together, they watched the flames burn until the fire was nothing but a fading memory. The witch was gone. And so was Andrew.

They had succeeded, but at a cost.

Chapter 22

Revelations

The truth was clear now—Tashi's presence still lingered, tied to the land by what remained of her body.

Isaac stood in the garden, staring at the disturbed soil and the fragments he'd uncovered. The bones, the cross—this wasn't just a burial site. It was something far more deliberate. He brushed the dirt from his hands, gripping the cross tightly as he headed back to the house.

Inside, Rudra and Jasper sat in the dimly lit living room. Rudra's shoulders were hunched, his head in his hands, his voice thick with emotion as he spoke to Jasper. "She doesn't even look like my daughter right now. She's pale, sick… but at least she's asleep. We didn't know what else to do."

Jasper, seated beside him, nodded silently, his expression thoughtful but tense.

When Isaac walked in, Rudra wiped his face quickly and stood. "What did you find?" he asked, desperation cracking through his voice.

Isaac met his eyes and motioned for him to sit. "This won't be easy to hear," he said.

Rudra hesitated but sat back down, gripping the armrests tightly. Jasper leaned forward slightly, his attention locked on Isaac.

Isaac started without hesitation. "Fifteen years ago, my brother Andrew and I dealt with something here—a woman named Tashi. She wasn't just an ordinary person. She performed rituals that tied her to this land and drew power from the people around her. Andrew performed an exorcism to drive out the spirit controlling her, but her body… it wasn't like anything we'd seen before."

Rudra frowned. "What do you mean?"

Isaac's voice was calm but heavy. "We couldn't bury her. We thought burning her body would sever her connection to this world. But that night, it rained before the fire could finish. We thought it was enough. We were wrong."

Jasper's brow furrowed. "And you think what's happening now is connected to her remains?"

Isaac nodded. "I found fragments of her bones in the garden. And this." He pulled the tarnished cross from his pocket, holding it up. "This wasn't just a grave—it was a ritual site. A tether. And when Arvi's blood came into contact with the soil, it woke up whatever was left of her power."

Rudra's face went pale, his voice barely a whisper. "Her blood…"

Isaac's gaze didn't waver. "That's what started all of this. Her blood touched the remains and reawakened Tashi's connection to this land."

Rudra leaned forward, resting his elbows on his knees. His hands covered his face as he spoke, his voice strained. "So what happens now?"

Isaac took a deep breath. "She's using Arvi as a vessel. It's not full possession yet, but it's getting closer. If we don't act soon…" He didn't finish the sentence.

The silence was heavy. Finally, Jasper spoke, his tone level but probing. "What's the plan? You said moving the bones could make things worse. So, what do we do?"

Isaac exhaled slowly, gripping the cross tightly. "We need to understand her. Tashi wasn't just a witch. Her rituals, her connection to the land—it's unlike anything I've encountered before. If we act without knowing exactly how she anchored herself, we could make her even stronger."

Rudra lifted his head, his voice trembling with anger. "And in the meantime? What happens to my daughter?"

Isaac stepped closer, his voice firm but steady. "We protect her. We keep her safe while we work. I know it's not enough, but if we rush this, we risk losing everything."

Rudra's anger boiled over. "Protect her? That's it? You're telling me to sit here and wait while she gets worse?"

Isaac's voice didn't falter. "I'm telling you we're not giving up. Not on her and not on this town. But you have to let me do this the right way. If we're going to save her, we can't make mistakes."

Rudra stared at Isaac, his breathing uneven. His hands gripped the chair tightly, his whole body tense. Finally, he leaned back, his shoulders slumping. His voice, when he spoke, was quiet, almost as if he was losing faith.

"If you can't save her… I don't think I'll ever forgive you. Ever forgive God."

Isaac met his gaze, his face heavy with understanding. "I know," he said quietly.

Rudra leaned forward, his head in his hands. "We're running out of time," he whispered.

Chapter 23

A Cry at Dawn

The stillness of early morning shattered with a sharp, piercing scream from upstairs. Rudra shot to his feet, his face pale with fear. "Arvi!" he yelled, already halfway up the stairs.

Isaac and Jasper followed close behind, their steps urgent but measured.

He set his hand on Rudra's shoulder, offering reassurance "Let me take a look," he said. "You've been through enough. Stay here for a moment."

Rudra hesitated, but Jasper's calm presence seemed to anchor him. With a nod, Rudra stepped back and let him through.

Isaac stood quietly behind them, his expression unreadable as Jasper opened the door and stepped inside.

The room was dim, bathed in the soft, gray light of dawn. Arvi lay on the bed, her small frame swallowed by the blankets. Jasper approached slowly, his movements deliberate, as his trained eyes scanned her.

Her face was swollen, her cheeks sunken, and her thin frame seemed almost skeletal under the covers. Jasper had worked with children in pain before, but this was something else entirely.

He knelt beside the bed, watching her labored breathing and the slight twitch in her lips, as though she were caught in a nightmare. His voice was low and gentle when he spoke. "Arvi… can you hear me?"

She didn't respond. Jasper reached out, touching her forehead lightly. Her skin was cold, clammy. He adjusted the blanket around her shoulders and sat back on his heels, his mind racing.

He had dealt with trauma before—seen children weather unimaginable pain—but this was different. It wasn't just her physical condition. The air in the room felt heavy, oppressive, as though something unseen was weighing it down.

"I'm not sure how to help you," Jasper whispered. "But I wish I could take this away."

He stayed for a moment longer, his trained eyes scanning her frail body. Her symptoms were alarming—malnutrition, swelling, and physical deterioration. It was clear she needed urgent medical attention.

This was a child in need of specialized care, a team of doctors, and immediate intervention. Everything about her condition screamed for a hospital bed, not a quiet room in a family home. Jasper felt his chest tighten as a sense of helplessness overwhelmed him.

As Jasper began to stand, Arvi's hand shot out, gripping his wrist tightly. He froze, his heart pounding as he looked down at her frail body. Her fingers, thin and cold, wrapped around his wrist with an unnatural strength that didn't match her condition.

Her grip wasn't just firm—it was unrelenting, almost painful. He winced as a sharp chill crept through his skin, seeping deeper with every passing moment. He tried to pull back gently, but her fingers refused to release, digging into his hand.

"Arvi…" he whispered, his voice shaking.

Her eyes remained closed, her face still, but her lips began to move. Then came the sound—a guttural screech, raw and inhuman, cutting through the air. It wasn't the voice of a little girl. It was jagged and primal, more like a wounded animal than anything human.

"It hurts… it hurts…"

Jasper's breath caught as her words echoed in the stillness of the room. The sound lingered, clawing at his mind, leaving him frozen in place. Slowly, her grip loosened, her hand falling back onto the bed, limp once more.

• • •

He stood there for a long moment, staring at her frail form. His chest tightened, his professional instincts warring with the growing unease that this was far beyond anything he had ever encountered.

At the doorway, Rudra turned to Jasper, his voice shaking. "What's happening to her?"

Jasper his hands covering his face as he tried to steady his breathing. When he finally looked up, his eyes were red, and his voice trembled with a mix of sorrow and anger. "She doesn't need a psychologist," he said, each word measured but laced with frustration. "What I saw… it wasn't human."

"Her body… it's breaking down. It's like she's been fighting for years, but whatever's happening—it's not just physical. It's something deeper, something darker." He paused, his voice shaking. "She grabbed my hand," Jasper said, his voice trembling. "It wasn't a weak grip—it was strong. Too strong for someone in her condition. Her fingers dug into my wrist like she was holding on for dear life".

Isaac took a breath, his brow furrowing as he considered the question. "The witch anchored herself to this land—rituals, blood, fear—they're all part of her grip here. Arvi's wound brought her into direct contact with those remains. That's the link we need to break. But to do that…" He paused, his gaze heavy. "We have to understand exactly how she's bound and undo it without giving her more power."

He stood silently for a moment, his jaw tight. When he finally spoke, his voice was low but firm. "The worst has happened. The witch has possessed her. She's using Arvi as a vessel to anchor herself back to this world." He paused, looking at Rudra and Jasper in turn. "We need to perform an exorcism to cleanse her soul before the possession becomes complete."

Jasper shot to his feet, pacing the room as anger bubbled to the surface. "An exorcism? And you're just now saying this? You're a priest—you do this for a living! And now you're telling me you can't save her?"

Isaac's expression didn't falter, but there was a flicker of weariness in his eyes. "I may be a priest, but I'm not Andrew," he said quietly. "I've assisted in exorcisms, yes, but leading one? Against a force this powerful? I'm not strong enough."

Jasper turned to him, his frustration spilling out. "Then who is? Do you think I can save her? I'm a psychologist! I deal with trauma, therapy—not ancient evil spirits!"

His voice was steady, though his hands trembled slightly. "You underestimate your role in this, Jasper. The child needs someone who believes in her. You may not think of it as fighting spirits, but your strength is what will help anchor her through this. You've seen what she's enduring. You understand her pain better than anyone here."

Jasper stopped, his fists clenching at his sides. "That's not enough, Isaac. Understanding her pain isn't enough when she's being torn apart by something none of us can fully grasp."

His chest heaving as anger as he said it, and disbelief churned inside him. He grabbed Isaac's car keys off the table without a word and shoved the door open, and stormed out of the house.

Chapter 24

A Test of Faith

Jasper couldn't believe what he had just heard. An exorcism? The priest wasn't even sure he could do it, and now they were looking at him? Jasper shook his head, his grip tightening on the keys. He'd severed his ties with faith a long time ago—when his father died, when all his prayers for a miracle went unanswered. He wasn't equipped for this. He wasn't anyone's savior.

Sliding into the driver's seat, he started the car and drove off, his knuckles white against the wheel. The gravel crunched beneath the tires as the house receded in the rearview mirror.

"An exorcism," he muttered under his breath, frustration simmering. "I work with minds, not ancient curses or supernatural horrors."

Halfway to town, Jasper pulled the car to the side of the road, his knuckles tight on the steering wheel. He leaned forward, resting his forehead against the cool leather, his chest heaving with everything he'd just witnessed. "What am I supposed to do?" he muttered, the empty road offering no answers.

He stepped out, the cool morning air brushing against his face as he surveyed his surroundings. The road stretched ahead, flanked by towering trees that swayed slightly in the breeze. The empty stretch felt isolating, the only sound the faint rustle of leaves.

Leaning against the seat, Jasper exhaled deeply, running a hand through his hair. The events of the past day flooded his mind— Arvi's frail grip, her guttural cries, the way her words didn't sound human. His breath hitched as he recalled the helplessness he felt standing in that room. He had prided himself on being the logical one, the professional, the person who could offer answers. But none of his training, none of his reason, had prepared him for this. Everything felt too big, too overwhelming.

He glanced up and down the road, hoping for some sign of life—a passing vehicle, a distant house—but there was nothing. Only the long, empty stretch of asphalt disappearing into the horizon.

His mind drifted to his father—Andrew, the man who had always seemed larger than life. The man who had dedicated his existence to helping others, only to leave Jasper behind with more questions than answers.

"I don't know how you did it," Jasper whispered to the memory of his father. His hands tightened into fists, his frustration turning inward. "You were supposed to have all the answers. You were supposed to show me how to deal with this."

The thought hit him like a blow to the chest: there was only one person he could call. One person who might give him some semblance of clarity.

Jasper pulled out his phone and immediately scrolled to the contact. Without a second thought, he pressed the call button. For years, he had avoided this conversation, but now, with his mind spinning and the moment pressing down on him, he needed to hear her voice.

"Jasper? It's early. Is everything alright?" He hesitated, his voice catching in his throat. "Mom, I… I don't know what I'm doing anymore."

Her concern was immediate, her tone soft but firm. "Talk to me, Jasper. What's happened?"

"I don't even know where to start," he said, his voice cracking. "I've been so angry for so long—at Dad, at God, at everything. And now, with everything happening… all that anger is falling apart, but I don't know what's left. If I've been wrong about all of it, then why did Dad have to die? Why did any of it have to happen?"

When she spoke, her voice carried both pain and strength. "Jasper, your dad didn't die in vain. He gave his life because he believed in something bigger than himself—bigger than all of us."

"But he put himself in danger," Jasper said, the frustration and pain bubbling up. "For strangers. For people he barely knew. How was that fair to us?"

"Because he knew his life wasn't just his own. And, Jasper, there's something I've never told you about the day you were born. You were born early," she began, her voice steady but filled with emotion. "The doctors didn't think you'd survive. You weren't breathing, Jasper. But your dad… he stayed by your side, praying harder than I've ever seen anyone pray before. He promised God that if you lived, he'd dedicate his life to Him."

Jasper felt the air leave his lungs, his father's face flashing in his mind. "He prayed for me?"

"Yes," she said gently. "And you lived. The doctors called it a miracle, but your dad… he believed it was something more. He knew you were saved for a reason, Jasper—for a purpose." She hesitated, her voice thick with emotion. "You were his miracle child."

Jasper stared at the floor, "Miracle child…" he murmured, as though the phrase itself was too big to comprehend.

His mother continued, "You were prematurely born in the sixth month, fighting for every breath. The odds were against you. But that night, in the hospital, something happened. Your father told me he saw a bright white light right by your incubator. He said the Angel of God touched you. When the nurses checked the next morning, you were breathing on your own. Your vitals were normal—completely healed. The doctors couldn't explain it. Your father knew in that moment that God had a plan for you. He never doubted it. He believed that all the trials in your life, even the hardest ones, were paving the way for you to fulfill that plan."

His grip on the phone tightened as her words hit him with the weight of unspoken truths. "Why didn't you ever tell me this?" he asked, his voice raw with frustration and disbelief.

"Because I didn't want you to carry a burden that wasn't yours," she said softly. "I wanted you to grow up with love, not guilt. But Jasper, for years, you've been holding on to anger that the devil planted in your heart. Your father didn't fail you—he gave everything for us and for God's purpose. He didn't die because of an exorcism, Jasper. You were four years old when he had open-heart surgery. The doctors warned us it was serious, that his heart couldn't handle stress. But your father… he was stubborn. He wouldn't stop. His work—helping people, serving God—meant everything to him."

Jasper's breath caught as the words settled in. "So… it wasn't because of what he did? All this time, I thought—"

She interrupted gently, her presence firm but loving. "No, Jasper. He knew the risks, and he chose to keep going. He didn't die because he failed; he died because he gave his all. He served until his very last breath, and I believe God honored that. Your father fulfilled his purpose, even if it cost him his life."

Her words cracked open a part of him he hadn't realized was locked away. "So… all this time, it's been the devil deceiving me? Making me blame God for what happened? Has god abandoned me?" His voice was low, almost afraid of the answer.

Her reply came without hesitation, full of certainty. "Absolutely not, Jasper. I've seen His hand in your life over and over again. The accident four years ago, when you walked away without a scratch—that wasn't luck. God has been protecting you, waiting for you to see it. The devil has been working overtime to make you doubt that truth, because it's terrified of what you're meant to do."

Jasper's heart raced, her words igniting something deep inside him. He thought of every moment he had dismissed as coincidence, every time he had felt like he was on the edge but somehow came through.

"Now tell me this, Jasper—should a thirteen-year-old boy hold anger toward God for something he couldn't understand, or should the woman who loved him for 24 years, who lost her partner, her everything, be the one to question God? I had every reason to be angry, but I wasn't. Evil didn't come for me—it came for you."

He was silent, her words cutting through the years of grief and bitterness he'd clung to.

"Evil deceived you, Jasper," she said softly but with conviction. "It made you believe God took your father away. But God didn't take him, and He didn't abandon you. Your father's story wasn't about loss—it was about faith. The devil twisted it into something else because it feared what you might become."

"You stop running," she said simply. "You take the first step, Jasper. Trust Him, just this once, and let Him show you what He's been preparing you for. You're not here by accident. You're here because there's work to do. And He's always been on your side, even when you couldn't see it."

Her words settled over him like a wave, washing away the bitterness he had carried for years. For the first time, he felt a lightness—not entirely, but enough for him to breathe deeply.

As the call ended, Jasper sat there in the stillness, the echoes of her words reverberating in his chest. A sudden clarity rushed through him, the pieces of his life falling into place in a way they never had before.

His eyes scanned the empty road ahead, but a distant sound pulled him from his thoughts. The soft chime of bells reached his ears, faint but unmistakable.

Chapter 25

Bound by Darkness

Back at Rudra's house, Isaac sat across from Rudra, who was slumped over, his face buried in his hands.

"This is why I called you," Rudra said, his voice breaking. "I don't know what to do anymore. That's not my daughter in there—it's the witch. Her behavior, her hunger… my daughter isn't in there."

He placed a hand on Rudra's shoulder. "I know this is hard to hear, but she's still in there, fighting. We have to act quickly before the witch's hold becomes permanent."

Rudra lifted his head, his eyes red and swollen. "I've seen things in the past few days that I can't explain. But what I do know is that she's slipping further away. Isaac, you have to help me. Please… save her."

Isaac exhaled deeply, his eyes clouded with guilt. "I've kept an eye on this place for years, knowing its history. My brother and I tried to banish the witch, but we failed to destroy her completely. I had to rush Andrew to the hospital after his heart attack, and we left things unfinished. Her spirit stayed buried in the soil, waiting."

Isaac hesitated, his voice heavy with regret. "If we had done more, this wouldn't be happening now. But now, we have to deal with the reality in front of us. We need to perform an exorcism."

Isaac stepped out of the house, heading toward where his car was parked. When he reached the driveway, he stopped abruptly, realizing the car was gone. A frustrated sigh escaped him. "Jasper," he muttered, piecing together that he must have taken it.

He didn't bother reaching for his phone. Isaac knew Jasper needed space—time to process everything—and deep down, he trusted that Jasper would find his way back. Adjusting his jacket, he began walking down the familiar path toward the church. Each step felt heavier, his thoughts circling back to Jasper's sudden departure and the girl lying upstairs.

Isaac approached the village church, his heart heavy and his mind racing. Inside, Nathaniel, a young priest, stood near the altar, rearranging a stack of hymnals. He glanced up, a faint smile crossing his face when he saw Isaac.

"Isaac," Nathaniel greeted, setting the books aside. "It's early. What brings you here?"

Isaac hesitated, running a hand over his face as he struggled to find the words. "Nathaniel, I need your help."

Nathaniel's demeanor shifted instantly. He stepped closer, his voice steady. "What's wrong?"

Isaac looked at him, the weight of the situation clear in his eyes. "There's a young girl. She's in danger. A witch's spirit has bound itself to her, and it's… it's getting worse, she's slipping away."

He paused, absorbing the gravity of Isaac's words. "You think it's possession?"

Isaac nodded. "I'm certain. And I need someone I trust to help me. You've assisted in exorcisms before. You understand what's at stake."

Nathaniel's jaw tightened, but he didn't hesitate. "I've assisted before, but never taken the lead. I'll do everything I can. Let's not waste any time."

Isaac placed a hand on Nathaniel's shoulder, grateful. "Thank you."

Nathaniel grabbed his bag and followed Isaac toward the door. There was no ceremony, no long discussion. Just a shared understanding that time was running out—and that together, they would do whatever it took to save the girl.

The three men entered Arvi's room. The air inside was heavy, almost stifling. The young pastor swallowed hard as he approached the bed, pulling out a vial of prayer oil.

He began pouring it in a cross shape around the bed, his hands trembling slightly. "Let us pray," he said, his voice steady but low. "The Lord's Prayer, all together."

Isaac and Rudra joined in, their voices blending with his. Jasper's absence was evident, but there was no time to dwell on it.

The pastor took out a small wooden cross and held it over Arvi's head. "In the name of the Father, the Son, and the Holy Spirit—"

Before he could finish, Arvi's body convulsed. Her eyes snapped open, though they weren't her own—pupils black, glowing faintly. Her lips twisted into a cruel smile.

"WAIT," she growled, the voice low and menacing.

The pastor froze as Arvi sat up abruptly, her movements jerky and unnatural. With a guttural laugh, she leaned forward and licked the cross.

The men recoiled in shock as she laughed louder, her voice echoing unnaturally in the small room. "You've been my slave all these years," she hissed at the pastor. "You think being baptized makes you powerful? You're nothing. And before I drag you to hell with me, I'll show you just how weak you really are."

Her body twisted, her limbs contorting as she vomited violently across the room, the acidic stench filling the air.

Isaac stepped forward, his voice trembling. "Arvi… I know you're in there. Don't let her take you."

The girl turned her head sharply to him, her smile widening. "You think you can save her?" she mocked. "She's already mine. I can see her in hell, dancing with me."

Isaac's faith wavered for a moment, his hands trembling. But he steeled himself, gripping his own cross tightly.

"We're not giving up on her," he said, his voice firm despite the fear in his eyes. "Not now. Not ever."

As if responding to his defiance, her body began to convulse violently. Her limbs jerked uncontrollably, and her back arched off the bed in unnatural spasms. Isaac and the pastor exchanged a panicked glance before stepping in.

"She's going to hurt herself!" Isaac said urgently.

They rushed to her side, each grabbing an arm to hold her down. Her small frame should have been easy to restrain, but the force of her thrashing was alarming. Her movements were erratic and powerful, her body writhing with an intensity that seemed impossible for her fragile state.

"I can't keep her still!" the pastor shouted, his grip slipping.

Isaac gritted his teeth, struggling to hold her down as she twisted beneath their hands. "We need to secure her," he said. "Now!"

The pastor nodded and grabbed the straps from Isaac's bag. With practiced hands, they tied her wrists and ankles to the bed frame, careful not to harm her but firm enough to stop her wild movements.

Arvi let out a guttural growl, her head twisting from side to side as the straps took hold. For a moment, she stilled, her breathing labored but even. Isaac and the pastor stepped back, their chests heaving as they caught their breath. Isaac closed the door behind them, locking it firmly. The muffled sounds of Arvi's strained breathing seeped through the walls, a chilling reminder of the battle still ahead.

The priest stood outside the door, his shoulders heavy with defeat. He pulled out a small vial of holy water, his hand trembling as he uncapped it.

"This room must remain protected," he said softly, his voice weary but resolute. He dipped his fingers into the water and began tracing the sign of the cross on the doorframe.

Isaac watched as the priest recited a quiet prayer: *"Saint Michael the Archangel, defend us in battle. Be our protection against the wickedness and snares of the devil…"*

"This has to hold," he said, though doubt flickered in his eyes. "For now."

Chapter 26

A Glimpse of Faith

Jasper, in his car, his breath hitching as he heard church bells. The sound was steady, as if calling to him.

It was faint but steady, drawing his attention. He turned, spotting a small church barely visible beyond the trees. For a moment, he hesitated, unsure why the sound pulled at him.

Taking a deep breath, he began walking toward it. The building stood quiet and unassuming, its wooden doors slightly ajar. Jasper pushed them open and stepped inside. The faint scent of candle wax and old wood greeted him. The room was empty, rows of worn pews leading up to a simple altar.

He sat down on the last bench, leaning forward with his elbows on his knees. His head dropped into his hands, the weight of everything pressing down. The screams, his mother's words, his father's legacy—all of it swirled in his mind. For the first time in years, he let himself feel the frustration, the confusion, and the anger he had buried so deep.

He wasn't sure why he was here. Maybe it was desperation, maybe curiosity, or maybe something deeper he didn't yet understand. His thoughts churned, and for a moment, he simply sat in the quiet, trying to breathe through the storm inside him.

The sound of footsteps broke the silence. He glanced up to see a man—a stranger—taking a seat beside him. The man looked ordinary, with kind eyes and a faint smile.

"Weekday, church—going through something?" the man asked, his tone light but knowing.

Jasper gave a small, humorless laugh. “Surely that applies to you too.”

The man chuckled softly. “Fair enough. But there’s no better place to be in times like these.”

They sat in silence for a moment, the quiet stretching between them. Then the man spoke again, his voice gentle but firm. “No matter how far we run, we always find ourselves drawn back to Him. Someone once said, ‘Seek and you shall find, ask and you shall receive, knock and the door will be opened.’”

Jasper turned slightly toward him, his curiosity piqued. “Is that supposed to mean something to me?”

The man smiled faintly. “It means you’re here for a reason. The devil doesn’t attack because you’re weak—it’s because you’re a threat. It knows there’s something valuable in you, something that can change lives. That’s why it deceives, to make you doubt your worth, your purpose.”

Jasper’s gaze dropped to his hands, his mind churning with what the man said. They weren’t far from the things his mother told him, but hearing them here, now, felt different. He felt seen, as though someone had peeled back the layers of his frustration and anger to lay bare the truth he had been avoiding for so long.

The man placed a hand on Jasper’s shoulder, his touch warm and steady. “God can use anything—even death—for His purpose,” he said. “The devil twists that meaning, but the truth always prevails. Remember that.”

Jasper glanced at the man’s hand and noticed a faint scar, almost like the mark of a nail. Before he could say anything, the man stood, offering a parting smile.

“May the Holy Spirit guide you.”

Jasper turned to call after him, but the seat was now empty. His heart raced as he replayed the man’s words. He stood abruptly and made his way to the altar, where the priest was lighting a candle.

“Father,” Jasper asked urgently, “who was the man sitting beside me just now? Where did he go?”

The priest looked up, puzzled. "Man? My son, you've been alone here for the past hour."

His mind spun as he whispered, "God can use anything—even death—for His purpose."

The realization struck him with force, piercing through years of confusion and anger. The doubt, the bitterness—it all seemed so small now. The pieces of his life that had felt so broken began to take shape, forming something he hadn't seen before.

Jasper fell to his knees in front of the altar, his head bowed. "I've been running," he whispered, his voice trembling. "I've been blind, and I've let my anger keep me from seeing You. I don't know how to do this, but… I trust You. I trust that You've brought me here for a reason."

He stayed there, his shoulders shaking as years of pain and bitterness poured out of him. The tears came freely, but for the first time, they didn't feel like weakness—they felt like release.

When he finally rose, his mind was clear. His heart still ached, but it wasn't weighed down by anger anymore. He knew what he had to do.

Chapter 27

Confronting the Shadows

Jasper pulled up to Rudra's house just as the sun dipped behind the horizon, painting the sky in streaks of amber and grey. The house loomed ahead, the flickering lights from inside hinting at the tension within.

The front door creaked as Jasper pushed it open, and the atmosphere hit him like a wall. The air was thick with unease, punctuated by faint grunts and muffled noises from upstairs. In the living room, Rudra sat hunched over on the couch, his hands pressed against his face. Isaac stood nearby, his arms crossed, staring intently at the staircase as if willing himself to take the next step. Nathaniel sat on a chair near the corner, clutching a Bible tightly, his lips moving in silent prayer.

Isaac was the first to notice Jasper. His shoulders eased slightly, and he motioned for Jasper to come closer. "You're here," he said simply, his voice carrying a mix of relief and urgency.

Nathaniel rose to his feet, extending a hand to Jasper. Their handshake was firm, but as his hand lingered briefly, he felt a strange sensation—a warmth that wasn't physical but spiritual. Something about Jasper's presence felt different, almost otherworldly. He didn't voice his thoughts but watched Jasper closely, trying to understand the man who had just entered the room.

"This isn't a coincidence," he said, his voice calm yet unwavering. "None of us are here by accident. Every step, every moment—it's been leading to this."

He took a step closer, his expression resolute. "I've spent years running from my faith, from my past, and from everything my father stood for. I didn't understand it back then—why he gave so much of himself, why he believed so deeply. But today… today, I saw it. I felt it, Uncle."

Jasper's gaze held firm as it met each of theirs, unshaken. "I grew up learning the prayers, repeating the words without knowing their weight. But now I understand. Those prayers weren't just words—they were armor. They were preparation."

He straightened, his shoulders back and his chin high. "God didn't just save me once. He's been shaping me for this moment, for this fight. I know why I'm here now, and I'm ready. Whatever that thing is, it's not going to win. Not today."

Isaac stepped forward, placing a reassuring hand on Jasper's shoulder. "Upstairs," he said. "She's restrained, but it's getting worse. We need to move quickly."

The faint grunting noises from upstairs suddenly grew louder, more guttural. Rudra flinched, his head snapping toward the staircase."

Jasper looked at Rudra, his expression softening. "We'll do everything we can," he said firmly. "But I need you to hold on. For her."

Rudra nodded weakly, his eyes darting between the men as they moved toward the staircase.

As they ascended, the sounds grew sharper. A low growl seemed to emanate from the walls themselves, a chilling reminder of the force they were about to confront. At the top of the stairs, the faint glimmer of a cross hung on the door handle to Arvi's room. It was meant as a safeguard, but now it lay on the floor, as though cast aside by an unseen hand.

Nathaniel whispered a quick prayer under his breath, gripping his Bible tighter as they approached the door. Jasper felt a cold sweat forming on his brow, but he steadied himself. He had been preparing for this moment, even if unknowingly, his entire life.

Isaac pushed open the door, and the sight inside brought the tension in the room to a boiling point. Arvi was strapped to the bed, her small frame jerking against the restraints. Her face was pale and gaunt, her eyes closed but her mouth twisted into an unsettling grimace. The room reeked of sweat and an unplaceable staleness that made the air hard to breathe.

“Hold her hands,” Isaac instructed, his voice steady but strained.

Rudra immediately moved to her left side, gripping her hand as though holding onto a piece of his daughter he refused to let go of. Isaac took her other hand, his knuckles whitening from the effort as Arvi thrashed violently against their grip.

Nathaniel stepped forward, pulling a vial of holy water from his bag. He began sprinkling it around the bed, murmuring prayers under his breath. “The Lord is my shepherd,” he said, his voice growing louder with each repetition, “I shall not want…”

The girl’s thrashing slowed, her head jerking toward the doorway as if sensing something—or someone. The room fell silent, an unnatural hush enveloping them as Jasper stepped inside.

Arvi’s head snapped up, her eyes flying open. They weren’t her eyes. Black and fathomless, they bore into Jasper with a hatred so intense it felt almost tangible.

“YOU FILTHY SERVANT OF THE HIGHEST,” she snarled, her voice guttural and layered with something unearthly. “WHY ARE YOU HERE?”

Jasper froze for a split second, her words struck him. He took a steadying breath, his grip tightening on the cross in his hand. *It knows,* he thought. *It knows everything.*

Before he could respond, Arvi’s demeanor shifted. Her expression crumbled, and tears streamed down her cheeks. She looked at Rudra, her voice breaking as she cried out, “Dad… Jasper is here to kill me. Please, Dad, save me! Don’t let him hurt me!”

Rudra faltered, his grip loosening slightly as he stared at his daughter in horror. “Arvi?” he whispered, his voice breaking. “Is it really you?”

“Please, Dad!” she screamed, her voice laced with desperation. “Save me! Save me!” Her cries escalated into a guttural roar as her body convulsed, the bed shaking violently under her.

"Don't let her fool you!" Isaac shouted, his voice cutting through the chaos. "It's not her—it's the witch!"

But before anyone could react, Arvi let out an ear-piercing shriek, her body snapping upright with unnatural force. With a burst of strength, she broke free of the restraints and hurled herself toward the window.

"NO!" Rudra yelled, lunging forward, but he was too late.

Arvi crashed through the glass, her body disappearing into the darkness of the forest beyond. The sound of shattering glass echoed through the night, followed by a chilling silence.

The four men stood frozen for a moment, coming to terms with what transpired.

"We need to go after her," Jasper said, his voice steady despite the adrenaline coursing through him. He turned to Nathaniel, who nodded, his jaw set with determination.

Jasper looked at the shattered window, the cool night air rushing in. He tightened his grip on the cross in his hand. Whatever lay ahead, he was ready, he wasn't running and he was here to fight.

Chapter 28

Sanctuary of Shadows

Jasper held up a hand as Rudra moved toward the door. “Stop,” he said firmly, his voice cutting through the chaos. Rudra froze, his panic giving way to confusion. Isaac and Nathaniel exchanged uneasy glances but said nothing.

“She ran because it fears me,” Jasper continued, turning to Rudra. “I wasn’t alone in that church. God was with me. The demon knows it. It’s why it’s trying to run—it knows whom I met today.”

Rudra opened his mouth to speak, but Jasper placed a hand on his shoulder, his grip steady and reassuring. “Trust me, Rudra. I will get your daughter back. I will bring her home. And I will send that thing back to hell where it belongs.”

For a moment, Rudra hesitated, his eyes searching Jasper’s face. Then, with a trembling nod, he stepped back. Jasper didn’t wait for further discussion. He turned and walked out, his footsteps purposeful as he disappeared into the dark forest.

This was why Jasper had been saved all those years ago. His father’s prayers, the near-misses with death, the encounter in the church—it all led to this. He couldn’t risk anyone else; this was between him, the girl, and the demon that had plagued this land for so long. He had to see it through alone because he finally understood his purpose.

The forest grew denser as Jasper moved further from the house. The faint light from the moon filtered through the canopy above, casting jagged shadows on the ground. Each step seemed to draw him deeper into an oppressive silence, broken only by the occasional snap of a branch or rustle of leaves. He gripped the cross around his neck, his thumb running over its surface as he pressed on.

The path felt strangely worn, as if it had been tread many times before. Jasper's chest tightened with the realization—she had been here, over and over again, and no one had noticed. The small disturbances in the undergrowth, the faint trace of footsteps—it all painted a picture of a secret routine, one hidden in plain sight.

Eventually, the trees parted, and the house stood like a wound in the heart of the forest, its walls dark and rotted, vines creeping up its sides. Jasper paused, his eyes narrowing. It wasn't just an old house—it was something more. Symbols were etched into the wood, their shapes sharp and chaotic, radiating an unsettling energy.

Jasper pushed open the door, its hinges groaning in protest. Inside, the air was thick and heavy, the faint scent of decay mingling with something metallic. His eyes adjusted to the dimness, and what he saw made his stomach churn. The room was filled with grotesque statues, their twisted forms frozen in expressions of torment. Symbols and markings covered the walls and floor, some smeared in what looked like dried blood. Above, crows hung from the beams, their lifeless bodies swaying gently, blood dripping into jars below.

Jasper's jaw tightened as he moved further into the room. The atmosphere pressed down on him, but he pushed it aside, his focus sharp. He scanned the space, searching for any sign of the girl.

A faint sound broke the silence—a laugh, low and guttural. It echoed through the room, coming from everywhere and nowhere at once. Jasper turned, his body tense, his eyes scanning the shadows. The sound came again, louder this time, followed by a scuttling noise. He caught a glimpse of movement—a blur darting from one corner to another. It was fast, unnatural.

"Arvi," Jasper called out, his voice steady. "I know you're in here."

The laughter turned into a low growl, and from the shadows, the girl emerged. She moved with an animalistic grace, her body low to the ground, her limbs twisting unnaturally. She climbed onto a large statue at the center of the room—a grotesque figure of a horned demon—and perched on it like a predator surveying its prey.

Her head tilted, and she grinned, her teeth bared. “This is my sanctuary,” she hissed, her voice layered with something ancient and guttural. “Where Belial blesses me every night. You’re in my domain now.”

Jasper stood his ground, his gaze locked on her. “That’s not you talking,” he said. “It’s the thing inside you. I’m here to send it back.”

She let out a sharp, mocking laugh and slithered down the statue, her movements inhuman. Reaching the floor, she crawled toward him, her nails scraping against the wood. Her voice dropped into a venomous growl. “You filthy servant of the Maker,” she spat. “Your soul is mine. You’ll feast with me in hell!”

Jasper tightened his grip on the cross around his neck, his knuckles white. “You don’t scare me,” he said calmly. “And you don’t own her. She doesn’t belong to you.”

Her eyes flashed, black and hollow. She lunged, stopping short just feet from him, her face twisting into a sneer. “You think your God can save her? This place belongs to me. She belongs to me!”

Jasper held the cross forward, his voice firm. “Not anymore.”

Chapter 29

The Final Battle

The eerie silence was punctuated only by faint whispers, words that didn't belong to this world. He closed his eyes for a moment, willing himself to focus.

In the depths of his memory, a scene played out—a conversation he had overheard as an eight-year-old boy. His father, Andrew, had been speaking with another pastor in their living room. Jasper had been seated at the edge of the room, pretending to read while eavesdropping intently.

"Submit yourselves, then, to God. Resist the devil, and he will flee from you," Andrew had said, his voice calm yet resolute. Jasper had spent days trying to memorize that verse, reciting it under his breath whenever he thought no one was listening. Now, the words came back to him with a clarity that startled him.

Jasper opened his eyes and reached into his pocket, pulling out his father's old notebook, the one he always kept close—a reminder of the legacy his father had left behind. The edges of the leather cover were frayed, the pages yellowed with time. Flipping through its familiar contents, his fingers stilled on a passage written in bold strokes:

James 4:7, "Submit yourselves, then, to God. Resist the devil, and he will flee from you."

A faint smile crossed Jasper's face as he reached for the locket hanging around his neck. Pulling it free, he unscrewed the small clasp to reveal the hidden prayer oil within. This wasn't just any oil—it had been given to him by Nathaniel earlier, blessed and entrusted to him as a sign of faith and strength. Jasper held it tightly for a moment, the weight of its significance grounding him.

Jasper stepped closer to the girl, who now crouched in the corner, her body twisting unnaturally. Her eyes glowed faintly in the dim light, her lips curling into a sinister smile.

"You think your prayers scare me?" she hissed, her voice guttural and layered with something far from human. "Your God has no power here."

Jasper ignored the voice, his focus unshaken. He reached into his coat pocket and retrieved a small diary, its leather cover worn and cracked. Inside, in his father's handwriting, was a powerful Hebrew prayer. It had been a cornerstone of his father's exorcisms, a testament to his unwavering faith. Jasper began to read.

As he chanted, he poured the prayer oil around the girl in a deliberate circle. The oil shimmered faintly in the flickering light, its scent cutting through the oppressive stench of the room.

With each word, the girl's body convulsed, her screams growing louder, more desperate. Jasper raised his voice, unwavering as he declared:

"Little children, you are from God and have overcome them, for he who is in you is greater than he who is in the world."

He looked directly at the girl, his voice steady yet commanding. "You're stronger than this, Arvi. Fight it. Say the words: 'I believe... ' Say it, Arvi. Over and over. Fight back."

For a moment, the girl stilled. Her lips trembled as her true voice broke through, soft and fragile. "I… I believe..," she whispered.

"Again!" Jasper urged.

"I believe…" she said, her voice growing stronger. **"I BELIEVE, I BELIEVE, I BELIEVE!"**

As Arvi repeated, the demonic presence inside her thrashed violently, its hold weakening. Jasper continued his Hebrew prayer, his voice unwavering as the dark force recoiled.

Suddenly, the door creaked open, and Isaac entered, carrying a bundle wrapped in cloth. The sight of the bones sent a chill through the room. "These are hers, the witch's bones" Isaac said, his voice low but firm. "What's left of her."

Jasper nodded, his jaw tightening. "Burn them. But wait until the spirit is out. If you burn them too soon, it could hurt her."

Isaac stepped back, cradling the bones as if they were something volatile and dangerous.

The air in the room grew thick, charged with an almost tangible energy. The girl let out a guttural scream as her body arched violently. Jasper didn't stop. He repeated the Hebrew prayer, his voice cutting through her wails.

The demon inside her snarled, its voice low and hateful. "You think you've won? She's mine!"

"Not today," Jasper said firmly, his voice like steel. "Not ever."

With a final scream, the demon was forced out, a dark, shadowy form twisting in the air before dissipating with a deafening roar. The room fell silent, save for Arvi's soft, labored breathing.

Chapter 30

Bringing Her Home

"She's free," Jasper said, his voice barely above a whisper.

Isaac didn't hesitate. He placed the bones in a small pit outside the house and lit them. The flames roared to life, consuming what remained of the witch's hold on this world.

Inside, Jasper knelt beside Arvi, gently supporting her frail body. Her eyes fluttered open for a brief moment, her voice a whisper. "Thank you," she murmured.

Jasper exhaled, a faint smile tugging at his lips. "You're safe now," he said, brushing a strand of hair from her face.

At that moment, Rudra rushed forward, his face streaked with tears and desperation. He fell to his knees beside his daughter, trembling as he carefully gathered her into his arms. "Arvi… my baby," he whispered, clutching her close. "I thought I'd lost you."

"She's free now," Jasper said softly, rising to his feet. "But she needs rest. Let's take her home."

Rudra nodded, his grip firm but tender as he held Arvi against his chest. Without another word, he turned and began walking away from the decrepit house. Jasper, Isaac, and Nathaniel followed closely, their shared silence heavy with relief and exhaustion.

As they stepped out into the night, Jasper paused and turned back. The house loomed dark and foreboding, its symbols and memories of anguish still etched into its walls. "No one else will suffer here," he said quietly.

Isaac, sensing Jasper's thoughts, stepped forward and struck a match. Together, they watched as the flames climbed higher, engulfing the house and reducing it to ash. The oppressive air that had hung around the place dissipated, replaced by the crackling of fire and the cool night breeze.

They walked back to Rudra's house in silence, the faint glow of dawn lighting their path. Rudra carried Arvi in his arms, her fragile body cradled close to his chest. Her breathing was soft, steady, but her pale face showed traces of the ordeal she had endured. Isaac walked beside him, occasionally steadying Rudra as they made their way home. Nathaniel and Jasper followed a few steps behind, their expressions tired but calm.

As they approached the house, the air felt lighter, a welcome change after the night's events. Rudra pushed open the door with his shoulder, carrying his daughter inside. The small living room, dimly lit by the first rays of sunlight, offered a sense of safety. Rudra gently laid Arvi down on the sofa, his hands shaking as he brushed the hair from her face.

He knelt beside her, his voice breaking. "She's back. My little girl… she's back."

Isaac placed a hand on Rudra's shoulder, offering silent comfort. Nathaniel stood near the doorway, his eyes scanning the room, as if ensuring nothing lingered from the night before. Jasper stepped forward, his gaze fixed on Arvi. Her chest rose and fell with every peaceful breath, a stark contrast to the chaos they had just endured.

Rudra turned to Jasper, his eyes red and swollen. "You kept your promise," he said, his voice choked with emotion. "You brought her back to me."

Jasper knelt beside Arvi, his hand resting gently on her forehead. "She fought too," he said softly. "God used her to fulfill His purpose. She was braver than any of us."

He leaned down and kissed her forehead tenderly. "She'll be alright now," he whispered. "She just needs rest."

Standing, Jasper placed a hand on Rudra's shoulder. "Give her some good food when she wakes up," he said with a faint smile. "She's been through a lot. I'll see her soon."

Rudra's tears fell freely, and he nodded, his gratitude unspoken but clear in his eyes. "Thank you, Jasper," he managed. "For everything."

Jasper turned to Isaac and Nathaniel, who both gave him a small nod. Without another word, he walked out of the house and toward the car. The quiet morning air surrounded him as he climbed into the passenger seat. Isaac took the wheel, and Nathaniel settled into the back, the three of them understanding the gravity of what had just passed as they drove away.

The drive was subdued, the hum of the engine the only sound. Jasper leaned his head against the window, watching as the world began to stir with the first signs of a new day. There was no celebration, no fanfare—just the quiet acknowledgment of a battle fought and won.

As they reached his house, Jasper stepped out and turned to Isaac and Nathaniel. "Thank you," he said simply. "For standing with me."

They nodded, offering no words, knowing none were needed. Jasper walked inside, the door clicking shut behind him. He stood in the quiet of his living room, the events of the night replaying in his mind. For the first time in years, he felt a sense of peace—not from the absence of conflict, but from knowing he had finally faced his purpose.

In the distance, the sun rose higher, its light spilling across the horizon, quietly promising hope and renewal.

Chapter 31

A New Calling

3 Years Later

The aroma of freshly brewed tea wafted through the house as Lizzy carefully arranged cups on a tray. The morning sun filtered through the curtains, casting soft patterns on the walls. Lizzy had settled into Kochi after leaving her life in Rome, where she and Jasper had first met during his visit for an interview with senior priests.

What began as a chance encounter over coffee at a quiet Roman café had grown into something neither had expected. Lizzy, a historian with a passion for ancient texts, had been drawn to Jasper's work and his unshakable sense of purpose. Now, their paths were intertwined in more ways than one.

Jasper entered the room, shaking off the weight of another phone call. "Father D'Angelo wants me to speak at a seminar next month," he said.

Lizzy handed him a cup of tea, her eyes sparkling with humor. "Looks like you're becoming quite the name in priestly circles."

He smiled, a hint of humility in his expression. "It's still sinking in."

Jasper's mother stood by the kitchen counter, her expression a mix of pride and amusement as she watched Lizzy. "You know," she began, handing Lizzy the sugar bowl, "his name has started spreading everywhere. That interview about the possession—it's all over the internet now. People are beginning to see what I've known all along. He was born for this."

Lizzy smiled, shaking her head as she added sugar to the tea. "He's so modest about it all. But I can see it—the change in him. He's grown into his faith in ways I never thought possible. It's not just the exorcisms; it's the way he carries himself, the way he talks about purpose. It's unshakable."

Jasper's mother nodded knowingly. "This is only the beginning for him. God has plans for that boy, bigger than any of us can imagine."

Lizzy picked up the tray and headed to the backyard, where Jasper often retreated for quiet reflection. He sat under the shade of a jackfruit tree, a Bible open on his lap. His posture was calm, but the furrow in his brow hinted at the thoughts swirling in his mind.

"Hey, you," Lizzy said softly as she approached, placing the tray on the small wooden table beside him. "You seem lost in your thoughts."

Jasper looked up, a small smile tugging at his lips as he closed the Bible. "Not lost," he replied, shaking his head. "Just… thinking about everything. About how I spent so much time running from this place, from my purpose. And now, being here, knowing what I know—it feels different. It feels right."

Lizzy sat beside him, placing a gentle hand on his arm. "That's okay. You were once lost, but now you're found."

Jasper chuckled, the tension in his face easing. "You always know what to say."

They sat together for a moment, the stillness of the backyard wrapping around them like a comforting blanket. Jasper's thoughts drifted to the journey that had brought him here—from his struggles with faith to the intense exorcisms in Rome that had tested every ounce of his inner strength.

Their quiet moment was interrupted by the sound of Jasper's mother calling from the house. She appeared at the back door, holding his phone. "Jasper, there's a call for you. Doesn't look like an Indian number."

Jasper frowned, getting to his feet, "It's European. Who could it be?"

Lizzy shrugged as he took the phone, his brow furrowing as he answered. "Hello? Who is this?"

On the other end, the faint sound of sobbing reached his ears, layered with an eerie, guttural noise in the background.

"I need your help," a woman's trembling voice pleaded. "Please, my daughter… she's in trouble."

Jasper's grip on the phone tightened as the unnatural noises grew louder. He glanced at Lizzy and his mother, their faces reflecting concern. "Ma'am," he said, his voice calm but firm, "please don't worry. I'm coming."

The call ended and handed the phone back to his mother and turned to Lizzy, who met his gaze with quiet understanding.

"You know what you need to do," she said softly.

He nodded, his expression resolute. "This is why I'm here."

Jasper disappeared into the house, gathering what he needed for the journey ahead. When he reappeared, his Bible and prayer oil were securely tucked into his bag. His mother placed a hand on his shoulder, her eyes filled with a mix of pride and worry.

After his first exorcism, Jasper had realized something profound—he was meant to save people. Psychology, he had once thought, was his way of serving, but this… this was the path God had prepared for him. And the love he had for children, something so innate and unwavering, now seemed like a gift from God—something given to keep him close to Him and God even before Jasper understood his purpose. It all made sense now, the compassion, the calling—it was never random, it was design.

Jasper gave his mother a reassuring nod and stepped toward the driveway. The path before him was daunting, but he knew it was one he was meant to walk.

"God is with you," she said simply.

Lizzy stepped closer, squeezing his hand. "You've got this."

Jasper gave her a faint smile. "I'm just His servant. He's got this," he replied.

•••

With that, he stepped into the driveway. This wasn't just another call—it was a continuation of the mission he now understood had been set before him long ago. As the car pulled away, Lizzy and his mother watched him go, their prayers wrapping around him like a shield against the unknown.

It was clear now: Jasper had embraced the calling that had always been his, even when he tried to resist it. He wasn't just following in his father's footsteps—he was carving his own path, one forged through faith, purpose, and the undeniable strength that came from knowing he was where he was meant to be.

This wasn't the end of his story. It was only the beginning of a new chapter—one where he fully embraced his calling and stood ready to face whatever darkness awaited.

THE END

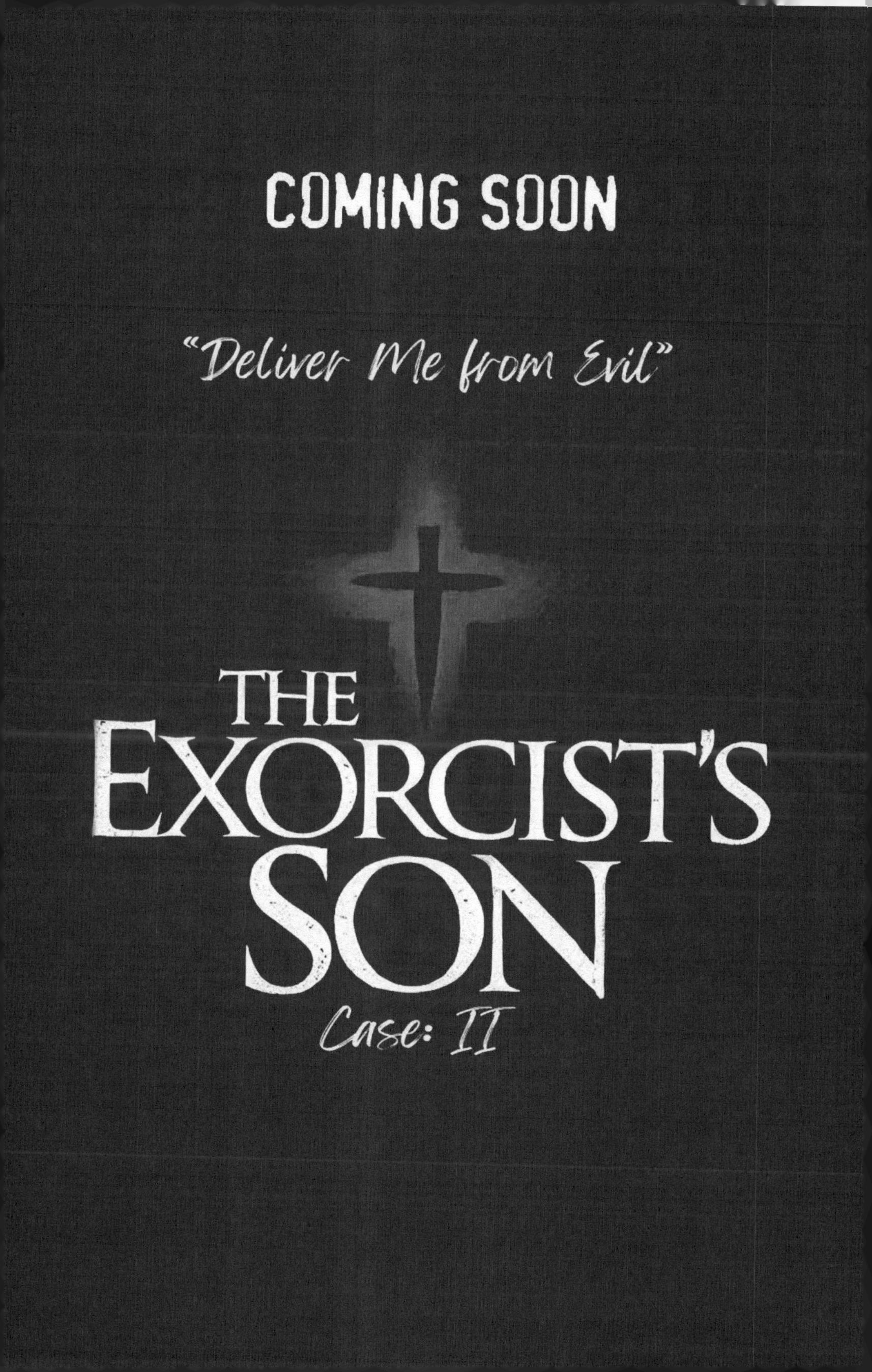

COMING SOON
"Deliver Me from Evil"
THE EXORCIST'S SON
Case: II

Printed at Repro India Ltd.